THIS MAN
COLTER

THIS MAN COLTER

•

Johnny D. Boggs

AVALON BOOKS
THOMAS BOUREGY AND COMPANY, INC.
401 LAFAYETTE STREET
NEW YORK, NEW YORK 10003

PRINTED IN THE UNITED STATES OF AMERICA
ON ACID-FREE PAPER
BY HADDON CRAFTSMEN, BLOOMSBURG, PENNSYLVANIA

For Lisa Smith,
My Publicist, Copy Editor, Sounding Board,
Best Friend, Wife and Love of My Life
—not in that order

Chapter One

Jeff Crutchfield laughed out loud when I walked into the adobe hovel at Borachio Station. "This," he told a man and woman at a nearby table, "is Colter, and he's wearin' every fabric known to man. Colter, you could be a walkin' advertisement for the Fort Davis sutler."

He was leaning against the makeshift bar, sipping mescal, Mississippi rifle by his side. Jeff was drunk, which was fitting. *Borachio* means violet—the station's named after the purple peak just south—but a few years back someone had scratched through the hand-painted sign over Rodolpho's place and scrawled *borracho* over it. *Borracho* is Spanish for drunk, and there wasn't a whole lot to do there except drink mescal, eat frijoles, and wait on the stage.

I gave Jeff a pleasant enough smile and walked to the bar, where Rodolpho was already pouring me a cup of coffee while Jeff finished his shot and refilled his glass.

Crutchfield's comments about my clothes didn't bother me. He was right. I wore calf-high deerskin moccasins, heavy fringed leather pants, a red wool

1

sash in which my Starr revolver and bowie knife were sheathed, white muslin shirt laced up with a thong, brown corduroy vest, green silk bandanna, and bone-colored hat.

Except no sutler would want me advertising his wares. My bandanna was frayed, moccasins worn out, pants stained with blood, grease and grime, and shirt and vest as old as dirt. The only thing new was my hat, which I had bought at Fort Davis two months back after losing my old slouch hat when a flash flood caught me by surprise in the Davis Mountains. The new one had a telescope crown, leather-laced brim, brown leather hatband, and stampede string. It cost me three wolf pelts.

I sipped the strong black coffee and looked around. The station was unusually crowded for midweek and the stagecoach wasn't due for two more days. Billy Haseloff and some of his daddy's cowboys from near Fort Stockton were playing cards in the corner and a Mexican in white farm clothes and a massive sombrero snored at a table; meanwhile a couple of the station's stock tenders slopped up beans with tortillas. And there was the couple, a young woman in gray riding skirt, navy blouse, and wide-brimmed hat, and a thin, gray-haired gent with a thick mustache who seemed to be trying to keep pace with Crutchfield's drinking. Actually the old coot looked as if he had lapped Jeff once and was loping behind about to pass him again.

"You wanted to see me?" I finally asked Crutchfield, and he gulped down his mescal and nodded, gesturing toward the man and woman.

"These are the McCarthys," he said. "They want to hire us as guides."

"Us?"

Crutchfield and I had scouted and hunted together before. He was an excellent shot and a good sort—prone to idle chatter though—and had a wife heavy with child down in Fort Davis. Unfortunately for her, he was filled with wanderlust. So was I. But I wasn't married and about to be a father. I was, however, pretty particular about my traveling partners. Jeff I didn't mind, but I studied the McCarthy duo intently.

The old man was glassy-eyed drunk and pale, almost consumptive-looking. He wore a dark suit and gray bowler. He definitely wasn't the outdoors type, and West Texas was about as out of doors as a body could get. The girl appeared to be in her midtwenties. She was tan, her dark blond hair lightened by the sun, and outfitted properly for the high desert. My gaze turned back to the man and I pursed my lips, contemplating him when I realized the girl was staring at me. She was sizing me up—just as I had done her. At this I had to smile.

Turning to Jeff, I asked, "What do they want?"

"We can speak English, Mr. Colter," the woman said.

I put my hands on my hips and glared at them. "All right, McCarthys. What do you want?"

"My daughter," the man said drunkenly, "wishes

you to take us to the Guadalupe Mountains where she can shoot a mountain lion. Then you can lead us to Franklin.''

I glanced at Jeff, shaking my head. ''You'll both be paid handsomely,'' the man said, but I turned without responding and finished my coffee. Crutchfield refilled his shot glass and waited.

''No thanks,'' I said. ''Jeff might take you to the Davis Mountains. You can bag a mountain lion there as good as the Guadalupes, but count me out.''

''Why?'' Crutchfield asked. He seemed shocked, though I thought he knew me better than that.

''Why?'' My voice rose with anger. ''I don't kill for sport. I kill to survive and to eat. Shooting a mountain lion just so you can brag about it ain't nothing I'll be a part of.''

''Mr. Colter!'' There was that voice again, strong but feminine, with a touch of a Scottish accent. She was standing, her blue eyes blazing as she walked toward me with a handful of papers and a small card. She handed me her card and laughed.

''I don't want to *kill* a mountain lion.''

I read the card:

G. W. McCarthy
Photographer
516 Fairmont Avenue, Boston, Massachusetts
Reasonable Rates, Excellent Service

Next, she placed six photographs in my hands, and I studied them. There was a shot of the Alamo in San

Antone, a couple of blurry looking soldiers on the parade ground at Fort Davis ("That's not very good," she said. "Those idiots wouldn't stand still!"), a Mexican woman carrying her infant in a basket, horses grazing by a river, a herd of longhorns, and a bunch of boats sailing somewhere. "Lynn Harbor," she said, and I returned the stack back to her.

I eyed the business card again. "G. W.?" I asked.

She sighed. "Gwendolyn Wisteria," she said, "but, please, just call me Gwen or G. W."

"Always thought Gwendolyn was a right pretty name," I offered.

"Not to me."

She took the card and continued, "No one, to my knowledge, has ever photographed a mountain lion in its natural habitat. I would like to try. And if we have no luck, I'm told the Guadalupe mountain range contains the highest peaks in Texas and is beautiful, unexplored country."

I laughed. "You think a lion's going to stand still long enough for you to take his photograph? If a couple of soldiers can't stay put—"

"Whether we see a lion or not, you'll be well paid," she said and, pulling a leather pouch from a pocket, spilled a handful of gold coins onto the bar. Crutchfield gawked, and I frowned and quickly put the money back in the bag and shoved it into her hands.

"Put that away!" I shouted and looked behind me.

The Mexican farmer was wide awake now, and Billy Haseloff and his saddle pals were staring at us.

So were Rodolpho and his workers. The sight of gold grabbed everybody's attention.

''Three hundred dollars,'' she said, and I felt like slapping her. ''A hundred now and the balance when we reach Franklin.''

''Shut up,'' I said and forced her back to the table. She gasped, and her face reddened as I made her sit down. She tried to rise, but my firm hand on her shoulder kept her seated.

''Don't tell me to shut up, Mr. Colter!'' she said.

''Ma'am,'' I said firmly but quietly, ''it ain't a good idea to go flashing around gold coin in a crowded room full of strangers. Not here. Not in West Texas.'' She seemed to understand, and I sat beside her. Jeff Crutchfield joined us, pouring Mr. McCarthy another drink.

''If Colter won't take you, ma'am,'' Crutchfield said, ''I can get you to the Guadalupes by myself.''

''Very well, Mr. Crutchfield,'' Miss McCarthy said. ''I don't think I care much for his company anyway.''

Great, I thought. Now I had to guide them. Sure, Jeff Crutchfield might get them to the Guadalupe Mountains, but he'd never get them to Franklin alive. That was tough, rugged country in the Chihuahuan Desert. Water was scarce; bandits and Apaches usually weren't.

''You'll need supplies,'' I said.

''We have plenty,'' she replied.

''It'll take ten days probably, just to get to the mountains.''

"Oh, I'd count on at least fourteen," she said. "I'm sure I'll see a lot of sights that I must photograph along the way."

"I wouldn't," I said. "You tarry too much, you'll be dead."

Leaving her with that thought, I turned on my heels and was out the door.

Chapter Two

"What is that?" I asked.

We were outside, in front of the station, and parked beside the corrals was the strangest-looking vehicle I had ever seen. It was black, sort of a cross between a hearse and buckboard, with a lot of luggage and a rolled-up canvas tent strapped on the top, a water barrel on each side, and a mule loaded with supplies tethered to the tailgate. Two other mules were harnessed in front, but the wagon was so heavily loaded its wheels sank deep in the sand, and I silently wondered if two mules could even pull the contraption.

I had used the back door, as was my custom, when I entered the station to meet Jeff, so I hadn't seen the wagon until now. It certainly was an attention-getter. Two gray-haired stock tenders and a Mexican girl maybe six years old were gaping at the thing. The girl reached out and touched it, then jumped back as if it were a rabid coyote, prompting a few cackles from Rodolpho's workers.

G. W. McCarthy laughed at my question. "You'd be surprised how many people ask that, Mr. Colter. The fact is, we even call it a 'What-Is-It Wagon.' It

8

contains our darkroom, plates, and supplies. We use a collodion wet-plate process now—you're probably more familiar with the antiquated Daguerrean method out here—so plates have to be developed immediately. We carry our darkroom in our wagon, and I have a giant camera plus a stereoscopic camera. When I sell prints in Franklin, I can make three-dimensional stereoscopic postcards, *cartes de viste,* 'Imperial'—''

G. W. McCarthy stopped suddenly, aware of the bewildered expressions Crutchfield and I were giving here. She could have been speaking Portuguese for all that we understood. ''I'm sorry,'' she said softly, and I do believe she was blushing, ''I get carried away sometimes.''

I probably would have smiled then, but her father stumbled past us, clutching a half-empty bottle of mescal in a shaky right hand, and staggered toward the wagon, shooing away the girl and stock tenders before he climbed into the back of the ''What-Is-It Wagon.''

''I don't mind a fellow getting roostered here,'' I told the woman, ''but I won't be stuck in the desert with some walking whiskey vat. Make sure your daddy understands that before we leave.''

Her eyes flamed. ''My father is not your concern,'' she snapped, pushed her way past us, and angrily strode to the darkroom on wheels.

I turned to Jeff, who smiled apologetically, drained his shot of mescal, and tossed the dirty glass onto the sand. ''I'm done drinkin', Colter,'' he said. ''I'll be sober when we leave.'' He hesitated a couple of seconds, then shyly asked, ''You figure out a split?''

Actually, I thought sixty-forty was more than generous—seventy-thirty was fair—but then I pictured Elizabeth Crutchfield down in Fort Davis with the baby about due. "Fifty-fifty," I said, "and you can take the entire advance if you send it to your wife before we leave. That'll give you fifty dollars when we reach Franklin."

Jeff nodded excitedly and asked when we would start.

The sun was dipping behind the Baylor Mountains to the northwest. There was no point in leaving until tomorrow, but I looked through the doorway at the crowd in Rodolpho's. I saw no reason in letting the McCarthys stay this close to Billy Haseloff and anybody else inside who would be tempted by the gold they had seen.

"Make sure they have enough grub and water and get them out of here," I said. "Camp at the dry creek bed a couple of miles west. Then meet me at Ojapite Arroyo tomorrow morning."

Jeff nodded, shouldered his rifle, and walked away. I tugged at the revolver in my sash, turned around, and went back inside to keep Billy Haseloff and his cowboy friends from getting any notions about robbery.

The excited chatter inside the hovel stopped dead when I closed the door. Billy Haseloff raked some silver and Yankee greenbacks into his hat and set it smartly on his head while the two cowboys he was playing poker with rose from the table and finished their bug juice.

Haseloff was a lean kid of maybe eighteen, about the width of a telegraph poll and almost as tall. He had stringy blond hair that fell to his shoulders from underneath a beaten, sweat-stained hat. Strapped to his right hip was a shiny Navy Colt, and he was reaching for his new Winchester "Yellow Boy" carbine when I stopped him.

"You boys calling it a day?"

Billy glowered as he and the two cowboys turned toward me. Haseloff's two companions were strictly working cowboys. They carried holstered revolvers—just about everyone did back then—but I doubted if they could hit a "What-Is-It Wagon" from fifteen paces. Billy was another matter, though. He fancied himself a gunman, and he never really liked me. If it were anyone else, I would not even worry about the two cowboys, but Haseloff's daddy paid them. So if Billy tried something, they'd be obliged to join in.

"It's gettin' late, Colter," Haseloff said stiffly. "Figured we'd head back toward the ranch."

"Long ride," I said. "I been helping out them blue-bellies and got some Yankee greenbacks to spend. Hope you boys will let me buy you a drink or three before you light out."

"Some other time, Colter," Haseloff said and turned to go.

My voice stopped all three of them in their tracks. "Now, you ain't gonna insult me by shunnin' my hospitality."

Billy swirled around, his right hand hovering over his Colt. The two cowboys turned as white as alkali. I was leaning against the bar, my thumbs hooked in my sash near the Starr .44, and looking as cool as a mountain creek. But that was a facade. Inside, my heart was pounding and my throat was dry.

"Colter," a voice said smoothly behind me. It was Rodolpho. "*Mi amigo.* If you must kill these hombres, *por favor,* do it outside. I do not wish to have to clean the blood off my floor again."

Good old Rudy, I thought. His statement took the fight out of Haseloff. The blood-cleaning comment was a good touch too, and fairly amusing considering that the floor was dirt. "There ain't gonna be no killin'," Billy said through clenched teeth. "All right, Colter. We'll drink with you." The three men moved beside me and we watched Rodolpho fill our shot glasses with forty-rod whiskey. The fat Mexican winked at me when he poured my drink. Rodolpho was the one man in the station who wouldn't have been tempted by the McCarthys' gold. He earned more than he could spend right here, selling lousy food and bad booze at outrageous prices.

Talk picked up in the room and I turned around, said something sociable to the nervous cowboy beside me, and sipped my whiskey. The cowboy asked me what I had been doing for the Army and I told him. Forts Stockton and Davis had been reoccupied by the Federals during the summer, and I was showing these newcomers where to find water at Rattlesnake Springs,

Hueco Tanks, and China Ponds when they were on patrols. The cowboy told a joke, and I laughed, but the grin vanished as I studied the room.

The Mexican farmer who had been snoring at the table when I met the McCarthys! He was gone.

Had I recognized the man, I might not have worried, but this was 1867 and Benito Juárez and his army had just routed and executed Emperor Maximilian in Mexico. The whole country was in an excited uproar, and some of the revolutionaries and defeated French mercenaries—really nothing more than bandits—were looking at Texas for some more fighting. Borachio Station wasn't exactly spitting distance from the border, but it was close.

Unfortunately, I had committed myself to drinking with Billy Haseloff. We had two more rounds. I chatted with the nearest cowboy, and Rodolpho discussed the art of cooking beans with the other cowhand. Billy didn't say one word. Finally, when the moon was rising, he finished his drink and angrily commanded, "Let's go home."

"Thanks for the drinks, Colter," one of the cowboys said. Billy glared at him, but I just smiled.

"Billy," I called out when he reached the door. He turned, eyes full of hate. "Make sure you do go home."

I followed them a ways, making sure they rode east toward Fort Stockton. I wasn't completely satisfied, but the Mexican farmer still worried me, so I turned back and returned to Rodolpho's. Besides, I had to pay

Rodolpho for the drinks and thank him for his help in defusing Billy Haseloff. Then I asked Rodolpho if he knew the sleeping farmer, but Rudy said he hadn't even noticed the man.

Frowning, I mounted my horse and headed to my cabin near Borachio Peak. After getting some sleep, I packed supplies—mostly powder, bullets, and grain, but also other necessities such as coffee, jerky, and chewing tobacco—and tried not to worry about the disappearing Mexican farmer or the possibility that Haseloff and his cronies had doubled back to find Jeff and the McCarthys.

Before daybreak, I was at Ojapite Arroyo. An hour later, when neither Jeff nor the McCarthys had shown up, I knew something was wrong.

Chapter Three

It didn't take long to find them. The "What-Is-It Wagon" was in a gully about a mile from our rendezvous site. Jeff Crutchfield sat cross-legged near his horse, holding his head and looking dazed. Standing next to him was Billy Haseloff, who was shouting at the McCarthys. A cowboy stood beside the driver's seat cradling Haseloff's Winchester repeater. G. W. McCarthy was yelling back at Billy, and her father sat glassy-eyed drunk on her right.

About twenty yards to the right of the wagon, parallel to Haseloff, I found another cowboy. He held an old Enfield musket, and three horses were staked behind him. I'm a self-educated man, so it didn't take me long to figure out what was going on. Haseloff and the two waddies had doubled back on me, waited along the road for the McCarthys, whacked Crutchfield on his head, and were trying to get the two Easterners to hand over the gold. G. W. was having none of that, and I figured it would just be a minute or two before Billy got more than testy.

Some folks say what I did was the bravest thing they ever heard, but when you look at it through my eyes, riding down there seemed like the best option. If I had stayed hidden in the rocks and called out for the three bandits to drop their weapons, chances are they would have started shooting. Then, most likely, someone would have been hurt, probably killed. So I trotted down into the center of things on Dollie, my brown-and-white paint.

Billy swung around quickly when he heard the hoofbeats and dropped his right hand on the butt of his Navy Colt. The cowboy with the Winchester jerked the muzzle away from the McCarthys and toward me, but he didn't bring the rifle to his shoulder, and his companion raised the Enfield a bit, like he was a Yankee soldier ''presenting arms.'' The weapons were ready, but nothing was aimed at me—yet. I figured that was because Haseloff fancied himself as a gunman, and the other two were working men who really didn't want to get into a shooting scrape.

Besides, I just bought those cowboys drinks, and it wasn't sociable to go pointing rifles at a gent who had treated you to a good drunk.

Anyway, I didn't stop until I was in front of Haseloff and to the left of the Enfield-wielding cowhand, keeping them at equal distances. The wagon was in front of me, but Haseloff obstructed my view of the boy with the Winchester. There was a method to my madness. Now, I'm no trick-shot artist, but I do have one fancy move in my repertoire. I had supplemented my income from the Federal Army by showing those bluebellies how it's done.

On horseback, I'd draw the Starr revolver from my sash, extend my arm to the right, and pull the trigger, hitting a can, bottle, or any target twenty paces away. Quickly I would swing the revolver in front of me while Dollie lowered her head and I'd shoot again, making another target spin or shatter. The Yankees kept betting that I'd miss, but I was sixteen-for-eighteen before they ran out of money—and one of those misses I did on purpose to make them feel better.

A Starr is a double-action revolver, which means I can shoot faster than anyone who has to hammer back a single-action Colt. The Starr is also a rather mean-looking weapon with a brutal cannonade, massive recoil, and heavy pull. I can accommodate for the pull, am accustomed to the recoil, and like its noise and looks. Fact is, a lot of people would rather stare into a double-barreled shotgun than a Starr .44.

So I had positioned Haseloff and a cowboy like they were targets. The third man, holding a Winchester repeater, was a snag in my plan and I'd have to figure out something on the fly.

"Billy, what do you think you're doing?" I said calmly.

"This ain't none of your affair, Colter. Ride out and you won't get hurt."

"Billy, these folks are paying me. And Crutchfield's my partner."

"I'm warnin' you, Colter."

In the corner of my eye, I saw G. W. McCarthy lifting a heavy canvas sack over her head. I didn't know what she was doing, but the cowboy beside her was turning back toward her so I figured it was time to start the ball.

I released the reins and drew the Starr. The waddy was just raising the musket to his shoulder when I pulled the trigger. There was a cry of pain and the whine of a bullet ricocheting off metal and I fired on Haseloff as Dollie lowered her head. Billy grunted as the bullet ripped the Colt from his hand. Meanwhile, G. W. smashed the kid's head with whatever was in the brown sack. Broken glass rattled; the cowboy dropped the Winchester and collapsed in a heap. The sack fell beside him, spilling shards of glass, and the young lady hurled out an unladylike oath and yelled, "My plates!"

I slid from the saddle and walked toward Haseloff, who was now on his knees, holding his mangled, bloody right hand. I kicked the Colt away from him and looked at the cowboy on my right. My bullet had smashed his Enfield as he was raising the musket and blown it apart. The kid was hurled onto his backside and was sitting up weakly now, ringing his shaking hands. The other cowboy was still out cold from the heavy sack of glass photographic plates.

"You all right, Jeff?" I asked.

"Yeah. Sorry, Colter."

"Miss McCarthy, Mr. McCarthy. Are y'all all right?"

G. W. replied, "We're fine! But I had to break ten unexposed plates and I am furious!"

I trained the Starr on Billy Haseloff's forehead and thumbed back the hammer for effect. "Would you like me to kill these men, ma'am?"

She apparently thought I was serious because she blanched and sat down quickly. "Heavens, no," she finally said. "Turn them over to your constable. . . ."

"Ma'am, the nearest civilian law is in Franklin. Out here we just do what's right and move on."

"No," she repeated, and I eased the hammer down on the revolver.

"Get up, Billy," I said dryly. "Give Miss Mc-Carthy your poker winnings from last night. We'll keep your new Winchester and your other guns too. That should cover Miss McCarthy's expenses and time."

"That ain't fair, Colter! That Winchester—"

"Don't preach to me about fairness. You tried to rob a woman and an old man. Most folks would shoot or hang you or at least drag you through prickly pear. I figure you'll get your hide tanned when you try explaining to your daddy about that bullet hole in your hand and the fact that you lost all your guns."

Crutchfield's knot on his forehead was more embarrassing than painful. "Billy just came in smooth-talkin' and friendly," he said, "then whipped out that Navy Colt of his. I should have expected something like that."

"Don't talk, Mr. Crutchfield," G. W. said as she applied some sort of salve to his injury.

I just watched. She was acting as if Jeff had saved her life and was fretting over that little bump on his head. Crutchfield would have hurt himself worse falling off his horse.

Mr. McCarthy put an arm around my shoulder. ''That was some fantastic marksmanship, sir,'' he said. ''Shooting the guns out of their hands rather than killing them. Straight out of a half-dime novel.'' He was slurring his words and his breath smelled of mescal. I wondered how a man could get drunk before the sun was even straight up. I was about to tell the man that I hadn't been aiming to wound, that the only reason those two men weren't dead or at least mortally wounded was because their guns got in the way of my bullets.

But then G. W. looked up at me with those big blue eyes and said, ''That was noble of you, Mr. Colter. I would not have wanted to see those men dead, highwaymen or not.

I shrugged and quickly changed my tune. ''Billy Haseloff's just sowing his oats, ma'am. No reason to kill him. He might turn out to be an upright citizen.''

''I sincerely doubt that, Mr. Colter.''

Well, G. W. McCarthy would prove me wrong about a lot of things, and Billy Haseloff was the first one. Because I doubt if he was still sowing his oats six years later when he robbed a bank and killed a teller in Fort Davis. They hanged him.

''Maybe,'' I told her, then motioned west to the desert. ''But where we're going, anyone we meet along the way will make Billy Haseloff look like a Methodist circuit rider.''

Chapter Four

I was sitting by the fire that night after supper, working on the weapons we had captured. The Enfield rifle had been smashed beyond repair, but Billy's Winchester was in perfect working order. It was brand spanking new. An update of the 1860 Henry model, it had gone on the market just this spring, and Billy's was the first I had seen. I was happy the rifle was in our hands, and not in Billy Haseloff's.

The .44-caliber rimfire rifle had a twenty-four-inch barrel, slide loading gate, and polished brass frame—hence the nickname "Yellow Boy," though we were calling it an "improved Henry" in '67. Weighing eight and a half pounds, it felt like a toy compared to the heavy cannons Jeff and I carried. Yellow Boy's magazine held an amazing seventeen rounds.

Jeff Crutchfield and I were used to single-shot rifles. Jeff carried a twenty-five-year-old piece whose heyday had been during the Mexican War, and I used a .58-caliber Springfield I had bought five years earlier. We could easily drop an elk at six hundred yards—and with just one shot we learned not to miss. A repeating rifle would come in handy in hostile country.

The revolvers were a Texas-made Dance .44, which I gave to Jeff, a Colt Dragoon .44 that weighed more than Dollie and kicked just as hard, and Billy's Navy .36. Some sand had gotten into the mechanisms when Billy dropped the gun after I shot him, clogging its works, and I was cleaning it when G. W. sat beside me.

"I didn't really thank you this morning," she said.

"No need to," I said and finished reassembling the Colt.

The fire crackled as we sat in silence, and finally I handed her the revolver.

"I want you to carry this with you in the wagon," I said, still holding the Colt butt-forward in my right hand. She stared at the weapon but didn't accept it. Her eyes looked up and locked on me. I began to plead my case.

"It's dangerous country. This is a good gun, doesn't have much of a recoil, and shoots true at close range. You and your father can handle it."

"I don't think so, Mr. Colter. Neither my father nor I am fond of guns. We're here to shoot photographs . . . remember?"

"Take the gun, Miss McCarthy," I said flatly. "Keep it under your wagon seat. You can at least shoot in the air as a sign of trouble if Jeff and I are out of camp."

Hesitantly she took the Colt and placed it beside her.

"It's ready to fire, ma'am. Just pull back the hammer, point, and pull the trigger. You can shoot five times before it's empty.'' That was providing the Colt didn't misfire, but I elected not to mention that. I didn't want to push my luck now that she had accepted the Colt.

She looked at me quizzically. "I thought they were called six-shooters."

I laughed. "You keep the hammer resting on an empty chamber, Miss McCarthy. So you don't shoot your foot off."

"Protecting us Easterners, eh, Mr. Colter?"

Gesturing toward my moccasins, I pointed out: "I have both feet, ma'am. I keep only five loads in my Starr too."

"You seem to know a lot about guns," she said. Her tone wasn't friendly now. I knew the McCarthys weren't comfortable with guns, and that didn't bother me. My mother had despised weapons—even butcher knives—but six-shooters and long guns were as much of a necessity as a hat and horse in West Texas.

I shrugged, and she was quiet again.

A blaze of light streaked across the black sky and disappeared a second later. Minutes later, another meteor burned a path toward Franklin, and I leaned back to watch the show. Flaming stars were easy to see in West Texas, maybe because the sky was so big and black at night, but meteor showers were fairly rare. I always enjoyed watching them; it was like a fireworks display on the Fourth of July.

"Tell me about yourself, Mr. Colter," she said after

a few minutes. She hadn't even noticed the shooting stars.

"Not much to tell."

"Well, what's your first name?"

I groaned. I never had been much of a talker, and she certainly wasn't going to get my mouth loping this way. But I was honest. "Raleigh," I answered and her response surprised me.

"Raleigh! How romantic and dashing."

"Colter will suffice, ma'am."

"But—"

"Gwendolyn Wisteria," I said sarcastically. I expected her to slap me or storm away in anger, but instead she just grinned. Firelight danced in her eyes.

"Touché, Mr. Colter."

Sighing, I began. "My mother met my father during the Runaway Scrape." Her expression was blank, so I explained. "During the Texas Revolution, after the Alamo massacre, everybody was fleeing Santa Anna's army. Folks just packed what they could and took off, trying to outrun the Mexicans, moving northeast right along with General Sam Houston and his men.

"Anyway, my dad was with Sam's army—if you could call it an army—and met my ma, wooed her on the fly, married her after a week, then went off and got killed at San Jacinto. My dad was originally from South Carolina. Someone told my mother that Raleigh was the capital there and hence, Raleigh Colter."

G. W. looked up at me shyly and said hesitantly, "Mr. Colter, I don't know how to tell you this, but, well, Raleigh is the capital of *North* Carolina."

"Yes, ma'am. I found that out some years later, and I reckon Raleigh Colter sounds better than Columbia Colter, but Colter is fine, Miss McCarthy."

"All right, Colter," she tried. "Let's make a deal, though, You call me Gwen. *Miss McCarthy* is too formal and the way you say *G. W.* sounds as if someone's pulling your teeth."

We tested each other's names, smirking, and then Gwen resumed her interview.

"So your father died before you were born. What about your mother?"

"She died when I was thirteen. Cholera."

"And you've been on your own since?"

"I worked as a stable hand in San Antone till I was sixteen. Owner and his wife helped me learn to read, write, and cipher. By then I was too bored to work in stables, so I headed west."

This was the most I had talked in years. Usually I let Jeff do all the speaking, but Gwen McCarthy was far from done with me.

"And just what is it that you do, Mr. Colter?" she asked. "I can't imagine you guide very many photographers to the Guadalupe Mountains?"

I smiled. "I do whatever it takes." She didn't return my smile. Fact is, she frowned. So I sighed and continued, "I've trapped wild horses, scouted for the Army, drove a team for the Butterfield line, hunted down wolves, worked cattle, done some trading. Whatever it takes."

"And I imagine you took time off to fight for your

grand Confederacy.'' There was more than a touch of bitterness in her voice. The war had been over for more than two years, but a lot of folks refused to let it die. Mostly Rebels, but Gwen's voice told me that the South didn't have a monopoly on bad feelings.

''No ma'am,'' I said, catching the surprise in her eyes. ''I figured that was none of my business. Bunch of politicians getting a lot of young folks killed.''

She sighed. ''More than you know . . .'' The meteor storm picked up and I watched. One ball of light raced a second and seemed to explode in silence like a Roman candle. Seconds later, another meteor took its place. Now, I had seen some light shows in my years, but nothing like this.

I gestured toward the sky, saying, ''Watch the fireworks, ma'am.'' She turned around and looked. Stars twinkled and the North Star shone brightly, but the meteors were quiet. Great, I thought, then a shooting star blazed forward and she gasped. We watched as more meteors rained from the heavens.

''Oh,'' Gwen complained. ''I wish we had the ability to take a photo in this light.''

I frowned. Now I liked photos well enough, but some things weren't meant to be put on a tintype. ''Do you have to see everything through a camera lens?'' I asked.

It wasn't meant to sound so bitter or mean-spirited, but Gwen McCarthy turned to me, rising angrily as she picked up the Navy Colt. ''It's better than seeing everything through a gun sight, Raleigh Colter!'' And she stormed away toward her bedroll near the wagon just as Jeff Crutchfield was walking toward us.

"You make her mad again?" he asked after squatting by the fire.

"I reckon so. She's a hard one to figure out."

"She's a female, Colter. You ain't never gonna figure her out."

Jeff hit the bull's-eye there. Because what he said about Gwen McCarthy has been proved right time and time again.

Chapter Five

 B y the next morning Gwen's anger had subsided.
We headed west along the old stagecoach road. Rolling mountains stretched before us toward the south-
west, looking like a dark sea in rough weather. When
we reached the base of that range, we would turn north
toward the Guadalupes, cutting between the smaller
mountains that popped up in this country like yucca.

This was October, or maybe it was early November.
I hadn't seen a calendar since talking to the post com-
mander at Fort Davis a month or so back. Rodolpho
had a calendar tacked to his wall, but it was seven
years old. Days and months were pretty much pointless in West Texas. Nor did seasons really matter. Oh,
you could expect flash floods in the spring and blue
northers in the winter, but the weather was unpredictable, both in the desert and at the higher elevations.

It was hot. Our horses kicked up yellow dust that
caked clothes, burned eyes, and parched throats. The
wind blew, but it was a dry, somber breeze that added
to the misery. Yet the McCarthys did not complain. I
figured they would be ready to turn back by now and
hightail it to New England, where the fall was pleasant

and colorful—at least from what I had read. But Gwen toughed it out and her father, well, he was probably too drunk to notice.

About midday we passed some medicine mounds, and I pointed them out to the McCarthys. The sun had sucked the energy out of them, but those small conical hills excited Gwen. She asked if she could take a photograph, and I relented.

I didn't see anything photographic about the three mounds. They were reddish brown, standing out against a backdrop of white and yellow, almost perfectly rounded and about six feet high. The Apaches and Comanches said they held medicinal powers, but Jeff and I considered them red rocks. I doubted if anyone would pay good money to hang a picture of them on their parlor wall. I knew I wouldn't.

Gwen studied the area first, then got out a giant black box and sat it on a tripod. Her father stayed in the shade of the wagon, sipping from a flask. Gwen muttered something about focal length and contrast, then said with a smile, "I need to give it some dimension. Colter and Jeff, would you mind standing beside the center mound?"

Jeff and I looked at each other dumbfounded. "It won't hurt, boys," she chided. "And I'll give you both a print. Please."

"Well, I ain't never had my picture taken," Jeff said. "What do I have to do?"

"Just stand still for about half a minute." She snapped a finger. "I'll tell you what. I'll take separate photos. One of you and one of Colter."

"You first, Colter," Jeff said with a smirk and stepped away from the mounds.

Shrugging, I positioned myself beside the rock. Gwen's head disappeared underneath a black cloth attached to the back of the camera. She ordered me to the left, told me to throw back my shoulders, then giggled.

"Jeff," she asked, "would you like to look through the lens?"

Crutchfield almost dropped his Mississippi rifle as he bounded toward the camera. Gwen helped him underneath the cloth, gave him some instructions, and then Jeff erupted, "Hey, Colter, you're upside down!"

They laughed, and Jeff came back into view, grinning sheepishly as Gwen went back to work. She inserted a plate into the camera, finally stepping toward the brass barrel in front of the box that held the lens. "Be very still, Colter," she whispered and removed the lens cover.

I held my breath and watched her lips count to twenty. Finally she replaced the lens cap and said, "You're all done, Colter. Now it's your turn, Jeff."

Jeff's smile vanished. It was like he was at the doctor's office to have a boil lanced or a tooth pulled. Gwen took his picture though, and then she disappeared into the "What-Is-It Wagon," saying she was going to develop and fix the negative. I heated up coffee and Jeff shared an afternoon drink with Mr. McCarthy.

Gwen didn't show us the photographs until that

night after supper. There I was, on a piece of paper about five inches by seven inches, looking like some cigar store Indian lost in the desert. Jeff cackled when he saw the photo, but I got the last laugh when Gwen produced his portrait.

His left arm was a blur because he reached up to scratch his nose. Jeff was a dark-skinned man from years in the desert, but he looked as white as hominy in the picture. He frowned.

"Don't move next time, Jeff," Gwen said. "I'll take a better photo of you when we reach the Guadalupe Mountains. Let me keep these prints in the wagon. You can have them back once we reach Franklin."

We returned the photos to her and she said she had to prepare more plates and left for the darkroom wagon. I sipped coffee.

"I look like some kind of monster." Jeff was pouting.

"Yep."

Crutchfield stormed away and I bellowed. Of course, I looked dead in my photograph, so I didn't have much room to laugh. If Jeff had had his way, he would have burned both photographs in the fire that night. Maybe that's why Gwen took them away. I'm glad she did, because those pictures would one day be our salvation.

A stagecoach passed us the next day. We pulled aside to let it pass, waving to the driver and shotgun rider as the coach bounced by and disappeared in a cloud of dust. The McCarthys were somber after the dust settled, and I knew why. That rickety old wagon would be their last look at civilization until we reached Franklin. In another day, we would turn north toward the Guadalupe Mountains.

That afternoon, Gwen said she wanted to take a stereoscope photograph of the mountains, pleading that the clouds were perfect and that she could use a yucca plant in the foreground for affect. I wasn't too keen about all this stopping for pictures.

Wild Horse Creek, as I had suspected, was bone dry, thus water would be nonexistent until we reached the Guadalupes, and I wanted to put this country behind us. But my hard stance wilted underneath Gwen's eyes. Jeff was out scouting for fresh meat, so we left Mr. McCarthy on the wagon seat and prepared to take a photograph.

The stereoscope camera was much different than the forty-pound black box Gwen used the day before. For one thing, it was smaller. Gwen lugged it on foot while I rode beside her. I offered to carry it, but she refused, probably because she was scared I would drop it, and I couldn't rightly fault that thinking. The camera was also red instead of black and had twin lenses in two brass barrels.

She set up the contraption just as she had done with the giant camera, placing it on a tripod and throwing a black sheet over the back of the camera box and her head. I tethered Dollie to some brush and watched.

While Gwen focused the camera, I cut off a chew of tobacco and sat down, pulling my hat over my eyes and finding the closest thing to shade in the hot afternoon.

Screaming mules snapped me out of my slumber minutes later. The "What-Is-It Wagon" was bounding right at Gwen, who yelled and stumbled backward in the middle of the road. The mule tied behind the wagon had broken its tether and bolted away, but it was the least of my worries. Mr. McCarthy sat in the seat, his eyes wide with fright, gripping the sides of the wagon with both hands. I yelled at him to grab the reins and set the brake, but the fool didn't budge.

Gwen scrambled to her feet and I darted forward, lowering my left shoulder and slamming into her, throwing us both across the road as the mules sent the fancy camera spinning and crashing to the ground. I felt the wind and dirt as the wagon raced past us out of control.

I found my feet in an instant. Gwen was short of breath, face colorless, but she nodded when I asked if she was all right. The wagon was ricocheting down the road as I flew into Dollie's saddle, kicking her in the ribs, and galloped after the drunken Mr. McCarthy and the runaway team.

Chapter Six

The latigo string was designed to keep my new hat from flying off my head while galloping. Instead, the wind sent my hat sailing, the braided rawhide catching under my chin, sliding under my nose, and finally going overboard. Expensive or not, the hat was the least of my worries.

Dollie was a fast horse, and the heavy darkroom wagon was being pulled by two mules. I knew they couldn't outrun me, but I was afraid the mules would break a leg or neck in a snake hole or the wagon would crash, spilling Mr. McCarthy, Gwen's expensive photographic supplies, and—most importantly—the two barrels of water onto the desert floor.

Cowboys seemed to have a prejudice against paint horses, though I never knew why. Dollie was fifteen hands high, hardworking and smart, and she could outrun most Texas cow ponies. The only difference between her and a waddy's horse was her multiple colors. She was brown and white, with four white feet and a small white star on her forehead. But a cowboy would rather walk than ride a paint horse, so I never had to worry about a Texan stealing Dollie.

Comanches, now, they were a different story. A chief from the Kwahadi band once offered me a Henry rifle, two buffalo robes, and his youngest and prettiest wife for Dollie.

As I chased the runaway wagon, I was glad I didn't take the Comanche's deal. Dollie galloped past the wagon, where McCarthy sat like a stone statue on the seat and his face as white as marble, and pulled in stride with the frightened mules. I took a deep breath and grabbed the nearest harness with my right hand, tried to say some soothing words to the mules—soothing ain't easy when you're bouncing in a saddle—and pulled on the harness while reining in Dollie with my left hand.

It was a gradual slowing process because I didn't want to scare the mules or get jerked underneath the wagon wheels, but eventually the animals calmed and, exhausted, finally stopped. Mr. McCarthy no longer was acting like a piece of granite. He jumped from the wagon seat and opened his carpetbag before I could slide from my saddle.

My anger was now out of control and I set upon him before he could get a pewter flask to his mouth in a shaky right hand. I slapped the container from his grasp and shoved him to the ground. In the corner of my eye I saw Gwen sprinting toward us, and far behind her Jeff had returned from his hunting trip and was gathering the stray mule. But I didn't care.

"You drunken fool!" I shouted, adding some choice cusswords for impact. "Do you have any notion what would have happened if we'd lost those water barrels? Or if those mules had been killed? Do you think you could walk back to Borachio Station?''

He reached for the flask again, but I kicked it into a creosote bush. "I said before that I won't travel through this country with a drunk, and I meant it." I picked up the carpetbag, surprised by its weight, and stormed to a nearby rock outcropping while Gwen, gasping, joined her father.

The contents of the battered old traveling case surprised me. Stephen McCarthy could have been a whiskey drummer with all the snake poison he carried. I picked up a bottle of forty rod pedaled in Fort Stockton, a homemade contraption that included corn liquor, Tabasco sauce, and strychnine. I smashed it against the rocks, grabbed another bottle, and did the same. There were two other flasks in the carpetbag, and these I poured out and tossed away.

We never really knew why the mules bolted. My guess is that Stephen McCarthy was too drunk to set the brake and while rooting through his saloon-in-a-carrying-case the noise of the bottles for some reason or another scared the team. Mules are hard to figure out. Maybe it was a rattlesnake. Maybe a combination of things. But all that mattered was that if Mr. McCarthy had remembered to pull back the brake lever, the whole episode would have been avoided.

Jeff rode up as I sent another bottle crashing against the rocks. We looked at each other without speaking, and I continued my chore. McCarthy had bottles of rye, mescal, and stuff that smelled stronger than coal oil. I found another bottle, broke it, and reached into the bag again. Jeff had dismounted and stood nearby as I stopped myself before sending this particular bottle to its doom.

The label caught my eye. I stared at it in disbelief. Unopened, straight from Scotland, it was a bottle of Glenlivet Scotch whisky, 1849. Now, I never knew my father or his heritage and had always considered myself a Texican. I didn't know if Colter was a Scottish, Irish, English, or Russian name for that matter, but I did know the value of eighteen-year-old Scotch in the Texas desert. I tossed the bottle to Jeff and said, ''Store this in your war bag. We probably should save it for medicinal purposes.''

I broke the remaining three bottles and dumped the empty luggage at McCarthy's feet. He was still lying on the ground, being comforted by his daughter. She shot an angry glance at me but said nothing.

''Reckon we'll camp here,'' I said. I wanted to put some more miles behind us, but those mules were worn out, and so were the McCarthys. I was calmer, so I knelt beside Stephen McCarthy and said, ''This is dangerous country. You could have killed me, yourself, and your daughter. You're paying me to get you to the Guadalupes and to Franklin safely. But I can't do that if you're on a high lonesome all the time. So your drinking ends. Now.''

Before striking out on Dollie to find my hat, though, I fetched the flask I had kicked into the creosote bush.

I wasn't taking any chances with McCarthy, so I began pouring its contents onto the ground. Well, I did stop for a second, and after making sure the McCarthys weren't watching, I drank the last three fingers myself and sent the flask flying. It had been a tough day, and I needed a shot.

Jeff's hunting trip had pretty much been a disaster, for all we had for supper was rattlesnake meat and beans. You won't find rattlesnake on the menu at Delmonico's, and there's a good reason for that. I've eaten turtle, locusts, even dog in a Cheyenne camp near Bent's Fort in Colorado, but rattlesnake is at the bottom of the list, even behind cooked cabbage. I learned not to be particular in West Texas, however, so I picked the little meat off the many bones and washed it down with coffee.

Gwen sat beside me. "You were hard on my father today," she said.

"He had it coming," I said. "How's your stuff?"

"The stereoscope camera's destroyed, some of the plates were broken in the wagon, but everything else is fine. I'm not angry at you, Ral . . . Colter. I was earlier, but you were right. I should have been tough on him long before now."

"I'm sure it's not easy living with . . ." I stopped myself. I was going to call her father "a walking whiskey vat," but for once my brain worked faster than my mouth.

"He wasn't always like this," Gwen said. "It was

the war. You didn't fight, so you really don't know about all the carnage and death.'' I didn't argue the point, and Gwen continued. ''Father was an established photographer before the war. He had a studio in Boston, had even written for *The Daguerrean Journal* and *The Photographic and Fine Art Journal*. And then came the Rebellion.

''Father took photographs with the Union Army, like the famous Matthew Brady, George Barnard, and others. He followed the Army in his 'What-Is-It Wagon,' at Bull Run, Seven Pines, Antietam. He even met President Lincoln and General Grant and took a portrait of them standing by a mortar. Then he recorded the aftermath of Cold Harbor, all the bodies. It was a slaughter. Our boys never had a chance. Ian had been killed in the charge there, and Father searched for his body, found it, and took his last photograph. Since then, he has been drinking himself to death.''

''Ian?'' I asked.

''My brother,'' she whispered.

I looked up. Gwen was crying.

Chapter Seven

Gwen believed I had been spared horrible sights because I didn't take part in the war, but she was wrong, though I let her think otherwise. After discovering a Kiowa camp wiped out by smallpox, Mexican sheepherders butchered by Comanches, and Apaches mutilated by scalphunters, I had seen my share of atrocities. Bandits and Indians had traded shots with me, and twice I had pulled my Starr in close quarters and sent my enemies to visit Saint Peter. These were not things I was proud of, but violence was a way of life out here.

Never had I seen a relative or even a friend killed in combat, and the thought of Stephen McCarthy finding his boy dead pulled at my hardened heart. I had read about Cold Harbor, where Grant sent his men charging to their death in Virginia in June of '64. Federal casualties totaled some seven thousand men to the Rebels' fifteen hundred. One of the officers at Fort Davis had fought there, and he told me that the Confederates called it ''Grant's slaughter pen,'' and even the mighty general himself, whom folks were already touting as our next president, admitted that it was his deadliest mistake in the war.

So Jeff and I took it easy on Mr. McCarthy. Oh, by no means would we let him have a drink, but we developed a softer approach to dealing with him, especially after a couple of days when the shakes hit. I taught him to chew tobacco, and he developed a passion for the habit, which seemed to take his mind off things, gave his mouth something to do, and helped curb his craving for food and hooch.

The heat must have topped ninety degrees over the next two days. Yes, this was fall, but it was also West Texas, and although I'm sure some readers will think this is just a fanciful tall Texas tale, I assure you it's the gospel. The sun took its toll on us, and worse, the wagon. By noon the second day, the left rear wagon wheel began to shrink and the metal tire separated from the wood. Both axles were beginning to screech for grease, so we were forced to stop.

Jeff volunteered to go hunting, though I doubted he would find anything in this heat, and to our surprise Stephen McCarthy asked to go along.

"Father, are you sure you're up to it?" Gwen asked.

Mr. McCarthy nodded and replied, "It would do me good."

So I let Jeff ride Dollie, and Gwen's father mounted Crutchfield's blue roan, who was less likely to throw an unprepared rider than my paint. They disappeared into the steaming white and charcoal mountains to the west, Gwen tried to find something resembling shade, and I went to work on the wagon.

The tire was the main concern. It was also the hottest job, so I tackled it first. I chopped up a creosote bush and got a fire going in a pit, heating the metal tire on the coals. I emptied the contents of my war bag into the wagon, then cut the sack into strips, let them soak in the water barrel and tacked the pieces onto the wheel rim. Next I placed the hot metal over the wet cloth. It sizzled and sealed.

I guess I learned something from my teenage years as a San Antonio stable hand after all.

By now my clothes were soaked through with sweat, but I kept at the job, putting the repaired wheel back on and greasing both axles. I was underneath the wagon, replacing the grease bucket when Gwen called to me.

"Colter, we have visitors."

I shot up without thinking and let loose with an oath as my head slammed into the wagon bottom. Crawling from under the wagon, I blinked repeatedly until the sweat was out of my eyes and I could see better. My revolver and knife, which I had removed before tackling my chores, lay on my bedroll, and I quickly shoved them into my wristband. Gwen had stepped away from the wagon, about ten yards in front of me, awaiting the two riders coming from the north.

Neither man I recognized, but they were white. One pulled a packhorse, and both rode in slowly and deliberately. There wasn't much I could do. The strangers would either be friendly or not, and we'd find out in a few minutes. It was too late to hide Gwen. Outlaws or not, the riders already recognized Gwen as a woman and I doubt she would have run anyway.

''Gwen,'' I said just loud enough for her to hear. ''If either man takes off his hat with his left hand, drop to the ground immediately. And no matter what, do not shake hands with them unless I say it's all right.''

''That's not very hospitable, Colter,'' she said without looking back.

''Hospitality ain't my strong suit.''

The lead rider was an older man, with white hair, a full beard, and spectacles covering the bluest eyes I had ever seen. A linen duster protected his clothes—despite the heat—and a wide-brimmed straw hat, plantation style, covered his head. I glimpsed the handle of an Arkansas Toothpick sheathed around his middle and was sure he carried a short gun in addition to the knife.

The other rider was in his midthirties, I guessed, with dirty brown hair hanging loosely from under a dusty Irish eight-piece cap. Two bandoleers full of brass cartridges crisscrossed his flannel shirt, and a Henry rifle was booted in his saddle. He carried two Navy Colts and a skinning knife belted around his waist.

Both men glanced at me, then looked at Gwen with a stare I didn't like. When the white-haired man smiled and swung from his claybank, I knew these men were no good. Camp manners require that a person be asked to light down before dismounting. The white-haired man walked toward Gwen while the younger ruffian stayed on his buckskin, holding the tether to his packhorse awfully close to his Navy Colts.

"Good day to you, madam," White Hair said, "and isn't it a scorcher!" His accent was hardcore Highland Scottish. Gwen shot a glance at me, but I didn't dare take my eyes off either man, not even for a second.

"It is," she said timidly, and then, trying to sound courteous and unafraid, added, "Definitely not what I'm used to in Boston."

White Hair slapped his right leg with a hard hand and shouted. "Boston! Your accent is Scottish, so how does a Scot come to light in that bastion of Irishmen?"

"My father is Scotch-Irish, but my mother's maiden name was MacGillivray and she was born in Scotland."

"MacGillivray! Aye, of the Clan Chattan like meself. It's an honor to meet a fellow kinsman in this blight of humanity." He held out his right hand and to my dismay Gwen McCarthy tentatively put forth her own hand in greeting.

"Gwen! No!" I shouted, and palmed my Starr revolver.

The smile on White Hair's face turned instantly into a frown, and he stepped away from Gwen and pulled a Remington .44. He was holding his lethal knife in his left hand—if he and Gwen had shaken hands, he would have jerked her toward him and put that knife against her throat—but this weapon he dropped and concentrated on killing me.

In the corner of my eye, I saw Gwen drop to the ground and cover her head as my revolver boomed twice. White Hair staggered back, pulled the trigger reflexively, and sent a lead slug into the ground, then collapsed without a sound. Pain shot through my right forearm and I fell to my knees, gripping my bloody arm with my left hand and dropping my Starr. Gwen's screams and the gunshots echoed off the nearby mountain walls.

The other man had slid from his horse and sent a .36 ball through my arm. I stared at my gun but couldn't move. My right arm was worthless now, and I couldn't have hit the wagon at fifteen paces with my left hand. I looked up at the other bandit, trying to think of something, but the pain was intense. Gwen, still covering herself on the ground, kept screaming. The outlaw grinned.

He was walking toward me, leveling the revolver's long barrel at my head.

Chapter Eight

At the last second I remembered my bowie knife, knowing it was too late. Irish Cap pulled the trigger, but the percussion capped merely popped harmlessly. Swearing loudly at the misfire, the man dropped the gun and reached for the other Navy Colt holstered on his left hip. By now I was moving.

I drew the bowie in my left hand, forced myself to stand, and charged the killer. Raising the knife to ear level, I planned to drive the weapon deep, but Irish Cap slammed the barrel of his second pistol across my temple. I dropped with a groan and a thud.

Rolling over, I looked up and instead of seeing Irish Cap leveling his gun at me there was Gwen cutting loose with something similar to a Johnny Reb cry, trying to force the Colt from the killer's hand. He was actually smiling as they struggled, but when Gwen reached up with her left hand and sliced his cheek with her fingernails, cutting to the bone, the smile disappeared and the man swore and sent a vicious left fist to her head. She whimpered and fell at his feet, and Irish Cap turned to finish me off.

I was on my knees, however, bringing my bowie

knife up with my good arm. Again the Colt's barrel came down, striking me across the forehead and once more I dropped, releasing my grip on the knife. My vision blurred. Blinking to refocus, I wondered what took the killer so long to shoot. Then everything became clear.

Irish Cap was no longer holding his second revolver. Instead both of his giant hands were wrapped around the hilt of my bowie knife, its blade buried just below the killer's rib cage. He slowly sank to his knees as blood poured from the gaping wound and seeped from his mouth. He looked at me blankly, then his eyes rolled back and he toppled forward with a sigh.

I felt furious. Struggling to my feet, I staggered toward Gwen. She stood quietly now and held her head. My right hand hung loosely at my side, the sleeve soaked with blood, but I gripped Gwen's shoulder with my left hand and shook her.

"I told you not to shake hands!"

She could only nod.

"This ain't a game! Those two would have killed us both, and you would have been a lot worse off than me!"

"I'm sorry."

"This ain't Boston! I don't want to die, and I don't want to see you killed! Why don't you listen to me?"

"I'm sorry," she repeated.

"You want to get killed? You want to see us all dead?"

Gwen's eyes flamed and she knocked my hand off her shoulder. ''I can only say 'I'm sorry' so many times, Colter!'' she snapped. ''You didn't say why I couldn't shake hands, you didn't tell me anything except some silly comment about 'hospitality ain't my strong suit.' And when I looked at you when those men arrived, you didn't give me any sort of signal! So don't blame all of this on me!''

She was right, of course. She usually was. As the McCarthys' guide, I had to make everything clear, and my failure to explain the situation had almost gotten both of us killed. The McCarthys were the greenhorns; I was the veteran frontiersman. I had no right to take my anger out on her.

Then I noticed her expression change. Instead of anger, concern crossed her face. ''Colter?'' she said softly.

It was only then that I realized I was on my knees. The heat, the head blows, and the loss of blood were taking their toll. Gwen was spinning before me, and I felt sick to my stomach. My head throbbed and the pain in my arm was brutal. I was falling, and vaguely heard Gwen shout my name.

I looked up after a minute and realized that she was cradling my head. Then darkness took over, and I fell into a deep, dreamless sleep.

Night had fallen by the time I awoke. My arm burned and ached, but I didn't look at it. I focused on the stars and fought back tears. If the bullet had struck bone, then likely Jeff Crutchfield had amputated my arm. Sure, I felt pain now but I had heard stories of amputees feeling itches and aches in limbs they no longer had. I was wrapped in my bedroll, near the campfire. I felt feverish and my head hurt. I was alive. But that was all I could say for sure.

"Colter?"

Gwen knelt beside me, forcing a motherly smile. She raised my head and gave me a sip of hot tea. Coffee had always been my drink of choice—since I was ten, in fact—but I must admit the tea was good. After a few sips, I drank the rest on my own, then placed the empty cup at my side.

"How do you feel?"

I wanted to say I felt embarrassed. I mean, these Bostonians thought I was straight out of a Beadle's half-dime novel, a fast-shooting and upright citizen who would not be fazed by a measly old arm wound. But the fact is that although I lived in danger, had killed men before, and had been shot at often enough, this was the first time I had ever been hit by a bullet. I don't think there's such a thing as a good, clean bullet wound. People die from loss of blood, of lead poisoning, of shock from amputations.

Embarrassed? Folks, I was petrified.

Gwen held my left hand then and squeezed it gently. "It's all right, Colter," she whispered, understanding. "You're all right."

"I'm scared to look," I said.

"Your arm's there."

Turning slowly, I saw my bandaged right arm. I

balled my fist. It hurt, and my muscles were stiff, but my right arm would be fine with proper care. Oh, it wouldn't be much good for a few days, but I was in one piece.

"Hey, Colter!" It was Jeff Crutchfield. He sat beside me and Gwen picked up the empty cup, saying she would bring me some more tea. Jeff watched her until she was gone, then turned to me and said solemnly, "You all right?"

"Yeah," I replied and nodded at my wounded arm. "Thanks to you."

He shook his head violently. "Not me, Colter. It was Miss McCarthy. I can skin a deer, but I ain't about to cut on no human, 'specially my pard."

"Gwen?" I was dumbstruck.

"Yep. She had a tourniquet around your arm by the time Mr. McCarthy and I got back here—we heard the shots. Then she poured half of that bottle we saved down your throat, the other half over the bullet hole. Good thing you had us keep it. It sure came in handy."

I didn't know if I should laugh or cry. Fine Scotch whisky used like that. I didn't even remember what it tasted like.

"Anyway," Crutchfield continued, "the bullet went right through your arm. Missed the bone, but you was bleeding something fierce, so Gwen heated up your knife and . . ." He cringed. "Well, I ain't got the stomach for it. What's it called? Cau . . . cau . . . ter—"

"Cauterize," I said.

Jeff nodded. "I buried the bodies," he said softly, then brought forth a leather pouch about the size of an Army canteen. "But I found these." Slowly, uncomfortably, he opened it and pulled out a grisly sight.

"Oh my goodness!"

It was Gwen. She stood beside us, holding a cup of tea, her eyes wide and face pale. Jeff quickly shoved the bloody locks of hair into the pouch and apologized.

Gwen composed herself quickly and knelt beside me, handing the cup to me but unable to take her eyes off the pouch. "Were they . . ." She couldn't finish.

"Scalps," I said. So the two men I had killed had been scalphunters, the lowest form of mankind I knew of. "Mexican government," I explained, "pays a bounty for any Apache scalps brought in, man, woman, or child." I turned to Jeff. "Bury those," I said, nodding at the pouch, "as far from those murderers as you can."

"It's horrible," Gwen said. "The bounty, I mean."

"Yes ma'am," I said. "And men like those we met don't care if they kill friendly Indians or not. You can't tell from the scalp. It's all black hair."

Gwen covered her mouth and nodded, then hurried away. I didn't tell her that those weren't Apache scalps. If doctored up, you couldn't tell a Mexican scalp from an Apache scalp either.

Chapter Nine

It may seem vulturelike, but we kept the dead scalp-hunters' horses and weapons, storing the small arsenal in the wagon and tying the animals behind the vehicle. That's just the way things were done on the frontier.

Gwen fretted over me more than my mama ever did, demanding that I ride in the wagon next to her. I didn't want to admit it, but she was right as I had lost too much blood to fork a horse under the desert sun. So Mr. McCarthy and Jeff rode on ahead, while I took it easy. Helping out matters was the fact the weather cooled off some. Oh, not enough to let you know it was November but at least it no longer felt like June.

"Your father is disappointed in me," I said that morning after Jeff and Stephen McCarthy rode away. It didn't take much to read that on the old man's face. He hadn't spoken to me since seeing the two dead men; he had even bummed chewing tobacco from Crutchfield instead of me.

"He's grateful," Gwen said. She had an easy manner with the team of mules, for which I—and my wounded arm—were thankful. "He has just seen too much death in his life. After you ran off those saddle hands without any bloodshed, he thought you were opposed to violence. And Mr. Crutchfield has been talking up your marksmanship, how you shoot those bottles and plates without even aiming.''

Shooting a revolver is more instinct than anything else. I was a point-shooter with my Starr, not from the hip, mind you, but without drawing a bead on my target. I was good at it, but it had taken years of practice. There was a big difference, though, in shooting at targets for bets and at killers to stay alive.

''Those bottles and plates aren't moving,'' I said. ''And they aren't shooting back.''

''I know. And so does Father, really. How's your arm?''

She was changing the subject, and I let her. I grunted something. She nodded. We rode in silence for an hour or so before she spoke again.

''You didn't want me to shake hands with those men, and I know why now. But what about the hat thing?''

''Another trick. Man takes off his hat with his hand to hide the movement of his gun hand. He brings it down slowly, covering his holster, draws his gun with his other hand and—''

''You've learned this from experience?''

''You have to read people out here, Gwen. Quickly. How he looks. How his horse looks. His guns. His eyes. Especially the eyes. You misread someone, it could kill you. I study everyone closely when I first meet them. It may seem kind of rude—''

Gwen interjected: "Like when we first met."

My head bobbed, remembering that day at Rodolpho's. It seemed a long time ago now, when in fact it was only a few days. I smiled at the memory.

"What did you think when you saw me?"

That was a dangerous question. Well, maybe the asking wasn't so loaded, but I knew I had to choose my answer carefully. I was honest, though. "You were dressed for the outdoors. You looked strong enough, determined." I smiled. "You were pretty. And then I noticed that you were looking me over, sizing me up. I knew right then that you were all right."

Gwen laughed. It was musical. She had smiled often enough, but laughter had been rare. And then curiosity got the better of me.

"What did you think of me?"

"That your blue eyes were amazing."

I had heard that before. Mexicans called the color "Tejano blue." It wasn't a compliment, though. It meant I had the eyes of a killer. Oftentimes I had gotten myself out of a pickle with a cold, hard stare.

"I guess you were what I expected for a guide, though," Gwen continued, "in your buckskins, that hat of yours. I have to admit I thought you quite handsome too. And then you kept talking and I said to myself, 'This is the most insolent man I've ever met.'"

The wagon jerked as the front wheel hit a deep hole. I wondered if Gwen didn't hit that hole on purpose, for added effect.

* * *

By noon, horseback riding in the desert had taken a toll on Stephen McCarthy. His face was haggard, reddened by the sun and wind, and his hands were trembling as he and Jeff trotted into camp on horseback. Mr. McCarthy immediately stumbled into the back of the wagon while Jeff unsaddled the horses and tied them to our string, replacing his mount with the scalphunter's claybank.

"Think your father will be all right?" Jeff asked Gwen after washing down a cold biscuit with canteen water.

"There's nothing in the wagon stronger than sour-dough starter," Gwen replied.

Jeff frowned. "That wasn't my meaning. He's had a hard go the past couple of days."

"He followed the Army of the Potomac for more than three years," Gwen said. "He'll be fine."

'Course, I thought to myself, *he wasn't a drunk back then.* But within minutes I heard McCarthy's soft snores. That night he even ate two helpings of beans, and the next morning he saddled a horse, although he rode near the wagon rather than take off scouting with Crutchfield.

Soon we were carrying on a conversation, as if he had forgotten the fact that I was just as violent as the soldiers he had photographed and as if I no longer recalled his early blunders caused by liquor.

"Magnificent country, Mr. Colter," he said, and I nodded. "Will it rain?"

Gray clouds hung above us with patches of blue appearing every now and then, but I doubted if water would fall any time soon. I shook my head. Rain clouds simply teased travelers in the desert, offering hope, but little precipitation. Gold grass, green yucca, and brown creosote bushes stretched around us, and the mountains to the west looked almost white.

''Are those the Guadalupes?'' he asked.

''No sir. We're about a day or two from the Guadalupes. Those . . .''

I stopped. Something glinted in those mountains. It was just a quick flash of something reflecting sunlight, and then it was gone. It could have been anything, but a gun barrel or pair of binoculars came to my mind first. Apaches? I glanced at the Colt revolver at Gwen's feet and tugged at my Starr.

''Those,'' I continued, trying to sound relaxed, ''are called the Sierra Diablos.'' I pointed to the rugged mountains toward the northeast. ''And those are the Delawares. Neither range is anything near as high as the Guadalupes.''

''I can hardly wait,'' Mr. McCarthy said.

That night, I helped Jeff tend the stock and told him what I had seen. He looked grim.

''I haven't seen any Indian sign,'' he whispered, glancing toward the McCarthys in camp to make sure they couldn't hear.

''That's what worries me,'' I said. ''If an Apache doesn't want to be seen, you aren't going to see him until it's too late, unless you're real lucky." I sighed and continued. "Chances are what I saw was nothing. But keep your eyes open."

"Colter!"

I had been studying the mountains intently. We were riding in the wagon the following day and Gwen had been talking. I hadn't heard a word she said. Her father had ridden off with Jeff that morning. I think Crutchfield would have preferred riding alone that morning, but he didn't want to offend—or worry—the Crutchfields. Besides, Stephen McCarthy was just as safe with Jeff in the desert as he was with Gwen and me in the wagon.

"I'm sorry," I said. "My mind was wandering."

"I could tell," she said. "I was asking you about Franklin."

Franklin never really impressed me as anything but a place to get a haircut or decent meal. By the early '70s, they had stopped calling the place Franklin and renamed it El Paso. It still didn't impress me, but neither did San Antonio or Austin or Sante Fe. I reckon I wasn't much of a city person.

"Border town," I said. "Fair size. Dusty. Got plenty of churches, bootmakers, and cantinas."

"Any photographer's studios?"

I shrugged. "I imagine. I never really looked for one. Why?"

"Father and I have to settle somewhere," she said. "We thought we'd try Franklin. If not there, we'd move on to Mesilla, maybe even Tucson."

That surprised me. I figured the McCarthys would take their photographs and then light a shuck back for Boston. Gwen laughed, reading my mind, and swept her arms at the heavily laden wagon and pack mule.

"You didn't think we'd lug all of this stuff on a vacation, did you?"

I didn't answer. Jeff Crutchfield's shrill whistle grabbed our attention. He was on a ridge about five hundred yards in front of us. I nodded at Gwen and she picked up the pace. I forced my right arm out of the makeshift sling and gripped the butt of my revolver.

Jeff and Mr. McCarthy had swung off their mounts by the time we approached them. I relaxed. Gwen gasped. Jeff hadn't been alerting us to danger after all.

Salt flats stretched to the west, more desert to the east. And towering ominously just north stood El Capitán, a towering mountain more than eight thousand feet high with a white, sheer cliff climbing the last thousand feet. Just beyond it, almost seven hundred feet higher, would be Guadalupe Peak and the rest of the rugged mountain range.

Chapter Ten

We camped by the old Butterfield Overland Mail Coach road at the foot of the Guadalupes that night, resting the animals before the long, tortuous climb up Guadalupe Pass. For six months I had bounced around while driving a celerity wagon, hauling passengers, baggage, and the mail over this very path till John Butterfield moved the line south in August of '59 so he could get Army protection and avoid the unpredictable Guadalupes.

I wondered if the "What-Is-It Wagon" could make it to the summit. There were times I made the Butterfield passengers walk up the steep grade to the Pinery Station at the top of the pass. Couldn't have made the trip any other way. I had been caught in sudden blizzards along the pass, and once—and this is gospel—the wind blew the bridle off Dollie.

Jeff would drive the McCarthys' wagon up the pass. I would have if not for my arm, but I'd pull the pack animals and Crutchfield's horse behind me on Dollie while the McCarthys rode the scalphunters' mounts.

Once we crested the pass, we'd rest the animals while I scouted the old stagecoach station. The Butterfield folks had abandoned the Pinery eight years ago, but it still got some use. I wanted to make sure if someone was staying there, they were friendly.

Jeff cracked his whip the next morning and the mules pulled forward. It was hard going from the start, and the gusting wind didn't help matters. Nor did the fact that the McCarthys had a two-mule team pulling an overloaded wagon. In my stagecoach-driving days there had been four horses or mules pulling my celerity coach—which, even with passengers, weighed a whole lot less than a photographer's wagon.

Near the summit, the mules faltered. Crutchfield yelled every cussword he knew, then made up some to keep the mules moving. If they stopped, we'd be hard-pressed to get them going again. I swung from Dollie, hobbled her forefeet, and staked the pack animals nearby, then dashed behind the wagon and pushed. Gwen and Mr. McCarthy soon joined me. We pushed. The mules pulled. Jeff shouted. The wind screamed.

My arm throbbed and my lungs burned. Suddenly Stephen McCarthy stopped pushing. He took a deep breath, then climbed onto the top of the wagon. *The fool!* I thought. Adding weight certainly wasn't going to help.

"McCarthy!" I shouted with a growl. "What do you think you're doing?"

Suddenly a wooden trunk crashed beside the wagon. The lock broke and the trunk opened, spilling its contents of books, magazines, photographs, and other personal items. A smaller trunk crashed next to it, and I knew Mr. McCarthy was thinking the way I should have been, lightening the wagon's load. Two carpetbags and a canvas tent came off next, and finally another trunk. This one also broke open, littering the road with corsets, camisoles, and other female unmentionables.

I glanced at Gwen. She blushed. As Mr. McCarthy climbed back down, the wind picked up and blew a pair of ruffle-and lace-trimmed pantaloons around my left leg. I tried to shake it off but couldn't.

Gwen, recovered from her initial embarrassment, laughed.

I blushed.

Finally we moved to the top of the summit and Jeff reined in the exhausted mules. Chests heaving, we staggered to the edge of the road and sat down, where I finally freed myself from Gwen's undergarment. It was cold up here, but we were sweating from the hard work.

Jeff set the wagon's brake and brought a canteen. I took a healthy swig and he laughed.

"What's so funny?"

"Now you know how your *payin'* customers felt when you made them walk up this hill," he said.

"Seldom made them push," I said, smiling as I rose.

"You can haul the stuff you threw over back up here," I said. "That was smart thinking, Mr.

McCarthy. I doubt if we could have made it otherwise. Gather up your stuff, load back up the wagon. The station is just up the road. We'll make it our base camp.''

I walked down the pass to where I had staked Dollie. After checking the loads in my revolver, I rode past Jeff and the McCarthys and cautiously toward the Pinery.

In its heyday, the Pinery Station stood like a fort at Guadalupe Pass, some fifty-five hundred feet above sea level. Three rooms with limestone walls and mud roofs were surrounded by limestone and adobe walls about eleven feet high and two and a half feet thick. There was a stone corral at the north end, a lean-to with a thatch roof where wagons were repaired on the opposite end, and beyond that a pine stockade.

Just northwest stood Hunter Peak, where I had killed some huge black-tailed deer in years past. Guadalupe Peak and El Capitán towered above us to the west, and the old Butterfield road ran east down the summit to Delaware Springs, Pope's Camp . . . all the way to Missouri.

A spring, about a quarter-mile from the station in a pine grove, provided the water, and the station hands had dug a ditch to the station so folks wouldn't have to walk so far for a drink. The stagecoaches pulled in here four times a week, changing teams and feeding passengers.

It was a good station—at least it had been eight

years ago when the station keeper ran roughshod over eight men, including a cook and two blacksmiths.

Now the walls were crumbling, the ditch filled in. Apaches had burned the station shortly after Butterfield abandoned it, and although someone had rebuilt the rooms during the war these had fallen into disrepair over the years. Dollie picked her way to the station yard and I hobbled her near some barberry shrubs, already showing their fall colors with yellow flowers and red berries. I palmed my Starr and went to work.

I had not set foot in the Pinery Station since the spring of '66 when I guided six scientists from the Smithsonian Institution and U.S. Geological Survey. They said they were interested in science, but I think they were looking for gold.

"There's no color in these mountains," the chief geologist told me after a week.

I smiled. "There's plenty of color," I replied. "Just not the kind you're looking for."

I walked around the yard, inside the station ruins, and scouted the spring, studying the ground for tracks or any other sign. Finally satisfied that no one had set foot in this station in months, I whistled and waited for the others to join me.

"Welcome home," I told Gwen as she studied the station. Then I barked out some orders.

"The corral looks to be in pretty good shape. We'll pen the animals there. There's a water trough, looks fine, and we'll fill it before we unhitch the team, then head to the spring and refill the barrel. Mr. McCarthy, you and Gwen can pitch your tent anywhere. Jeff and I will throw up a tent here. Then—''

''Colter?'' It was Gwen. She stared longingly at the station's rooms.

''Can't we sleep inside, under a real roof?''

I studied the old station again. It's funny what a week or so of traveling in the desert will do to a body. Gwen looked at the Pinery as if it were some fine Boston hotel. I had a pretty good imagination but I never would call that mud and thatch ''a real roof.''

''Gwen,'' I explained, ''the rooms haven't been used in at least a year. They're probably full of rattlesnakes, and I'd hate to heat up the rooms and wake up in the morning covered with diamondbacks.''

She sighed and relented without argument. I reckon we could have cleaned the rooms out first and chased out or killed any rattlers, but I was never much good at housecleaning. So we completed our chores and got settled in just before dusk.

Up until now we had slept under the stars in bedrolls, but since we'd be staying a week or so in the mountains, where it got cold and windy, we opted for the protection of canvas tents. The McCarthys had a wall tent about ten feet wide and eight feet long. Jeff and I crammed into a five-by-seven Army wedge tent. Crutchfield said he won the tent in a poker game back in '62, but I think he stole it during General Sibley's retreat after the Confederates' failed invasion of New Mexico.

No matter. I should have listened to Gwen.

Chapter Eleven

Supper went down our gullets quickly and we retired to our tents in a hurry. Not because we were exhausted, mind you, but the wind was blowing something fierce. Back in '66 one of those government scientists had measured gusts in these mountains at seventy-seven miles per hour. It was cold. Bitterly cold.

Our spirits plummeted with the temperature. I crawled into the tent, pulled my soogans over my head, and tried to get some shut-eye. But the wind made that canvas tent pop like the Fourth of July in Philadelphia. Wolves howled above the wind. Worst of all, though, was Jeff Crutchfield's snoring.

I don't know how his wife puts up with it, or maybe that's why she lets him go off gallivanting across the countryside. Sleeping outside, his snores weren't so bad, but this was the first time I had ever shared a tent with him. Jeff stood about six foot two, two inches taller than me, though I outweighed him by ten or fifteen pounds. But for a skinny cuss, he could sure snore up a storm.

For hours I tossed and turned, but the wind kept

picking up, the air got colder, and Jeff's snores never ceased. I sat up in the middle of the night, grumbled, and changed positions so that my head was by his feet and away from his mouth and nose. I had hoped to wake him up but had no such luck. Of course, now my head was by the tent flap, which although tied down still let in frigid gusts. Again I pulled the blankets over my head and squeezed my eyes shut, sniffling and shaking—and swearing underneath my frosty breath.

At some point Crutchfield stopped snoring and I drifted off to sleep. Before I could dream of Rodolpho's chili or something even warmer, I woke up with a start. Jeff was snoring again. That's enough, I said to myself, pulled my right arm from underneath the soogans, and slapped Crutchfield's thigh. He grunted something and rolled over and the snoring ceased once more.

I gave thanks and tried to get to sleep before the racket resumed.

By dawn the wind had died down, though it was still frigid. Jeff was sleeping peacefully now, but I was freezing. I pulled on my coat, unfastened the tent, and stepped outside. The air was clear, the land, tents, and wagon covered with frost. The cook fire had gone out during the night. I swore and gathered some dry twigs and limbs and soon had a small blaze going. Then I grabbed the coffeepot and tried to pour a cup, but it was frozen solid. After warming my hands, I set the frozen, frost-covered blue pot on the fire and checked on the livestock.

The water in the corral's trough was covered with ice, but I cracked it with my bowie knife. I wiped my nose and got ready to cook breakfast.

The sun was slowly climbing over the mountains by the time Crutchfield and the McCarthys rose. I snared a rabbit by the corral, skinned and cleaned it, and had fresh meat sizzling in a frying pan, and the once-frozen coffee steaming. Sourdough biscuits were browning in the Dutch oven, and I had gathered a cupful of barberries to make jelly for supper.

I was pretty pleased with myself, having accomplished all of this with next-to-zero sleep.

"Good morning," I said cheerily.

Gwen's eyes were burning. "Can't we *please* sleep in the station?"

Jeff took off hunting after breakfast while I made myself busy cleaning our captured arsenal and crushing berries in a coffee cup. I did check the dusty rooms in the station, but I wasn't about to move inside yet. If Gwen wanted a roof over her head, she could sleep in the cot in her "What-Is-It Wagon." I was convinced there were thousands of rattlers in that old building just waiting to get me.

It's not that I was deathly afraid of snakes, mind you. Rattlesnakes eat mice and vermin and play an important part in the wilds of Texas; I just don't want any part of them.

Mr. McCarthy had the shakes again. He went through a plug of tobacco like a beaver through a sapling, drank about a gallon of coffee, and walked up and down the road, just trying to stay busy. I felt sorry for the guy but knew there was nothing I could do for him; he was fighting his own personal demons.

Gwen loaded her camera and supplies on the pack mule and headed toward Guadalupe Peak. I told her to stay close, and she assured me that she had no intention of climbing the mountain today.

For once, she listened to me. She came back that afternoon smiling, praising the country and saying she had taken some breathtaking photographs of the peak. It was warmer, you see. I figured that around sunset, when the wind picked up and the cold moved in again, she would be just as ornery as ever.

"You going to make some prints?" I asked as I reassembled a Colt's revolving rifle that had belonged to one of the scalphunters.

"Are you trying to get rid of me, Colter?"

"Not at all."

She smiled. "No," she replied. "I can do prints in my wagon, but it's better to work in a studio's darkroom. Besides, I don't have much paper to print on. I hope to find a studio in Franklin. How's your arm?"

I clenched my fist and flexed my arm twice. It was still a little stiff but I lied. "As good as new."

"So when do we go after a mountain lion?"

I looked at her blankly. "That is why we came here, remember? I want to photograph a mountain lion in the wild."

"I'll scout out a place tomorrow." I was making

this up as I went. No one had ever photographed a lion, I figured, because it's next to impossible. Cats were hard to find. I supposed I could have caught a deer, hamstrung it, and picketed it near a water hole, but I doubted if Gwen would tolerate that cruelty. Besides, we'd probably only attract wolves and ravens. But she was paying me good money to try and find a puma, so I figured I'd have to try. I had until tomorrow to think of something.

Jeff came back an hour later with a fine elk he shot near Manzanita Spring, northeast of our camp. He hoisted the carcass over a tree limb, sliced out a hind quarter, and we prepared a feast: roast elk, sourdough biscuits with barberry jelly, wild onions, and coffee.

Stuffed, we turned in at dusk. I was asleep before Jeff could start snoring.

I awoke with a start in the middle of the night. The horses and mules were screaming from the corrals. Something outside grunted, and my right hand instinctively found the Starr revolver. Jeff was up too, cocking the Mississippi rifle he always kept nearby.

"Apaches?" he whispered.

There was only one way to find out. We moved quickly but cautiously out of the tent. The fire was still going, but clouds blocked any light from the moon and stars. Muffled voices sounded nearby, but we recognized the McCarthys. Jeff crept toward the crying livestock, while I moved around the other side.

My eyes grew accustomed to the darkness, and I

noticed a figure in front of me near a tree. Another grunt sounded, then something dashed toward the McCarthys' tent as the flap opened. Gwen screamed and bolted away. Something snorted.

Apaches don't make that much noise, I thought, and as the figure in front of me turned around and stepped near the glowing campfire I realized this was no Apache and froze.

I had no idea where Gwen had gone, and, truthfully, I didn't care. My eyes locked on the eight-foot-tall, seven-hundred-plus-pound grizzly bear just spitting distance from me. It roared as I glanced at the useless Starr revolver in my right hand. A .44 wouldn't faze a bear, especially this mean ma who had a craving for the elk we stupidly left hanging from the tree.

In the corner of my eye, Mr. McCarthy yelled something as another dark figure roared and ran back toward me. Another figure followed close behind, knocking over poles, tripping twine, and causing the tent to collapse on Stephen McCarthy.

Two cubs hid behind their mother. My lungs stopped. Sweat trickled down my forehead. Mr. McCarthy swore and shouted from underneath the fallen tent above the din of the panicked livestock. The mother bear let out a deafening roar—and charged.

Bears are unbelievably fast animals. A human can't outrun one. But I sure tried.

Tossing away my Starr I dashed across our camp toward the stagecoach station. The clouds moved and a ray of moonlight helped my vision. I lunged for the building's roof and tried to pull myself up as the bear lashed out, ripping off my left moccasin. I scrambled onto the roof as the bear placed her thick front feet and long claws in front of my face.

Then I saw Gwen. She had picked up the Colt's revolving rifle and was trying to sneak up behind the bear. The rifle was basically just a Colt's pistol on a long gun's frame—about as useless on a grizzly as my pocket knife. But the rifle Gwen held was even more worthless because it wasn't even loaded. As Gwen pulled back the hammer, I yelled, "No! Gwen! No!"

She pulled the trigger as the bear turned to face her. The hammer clicked on an empty chamber, and Gwen's eyes bulged as the grizzly sprinted toward her. Gwen dropped the rifle and stood straight, frozen in terror. The bear stopped and rose on her hind legs, towering over Gwen and letting out a furious roar. One swipe of the paw, and I'd bury that woman in these mountains, so I dropped from the roof, although I had no idea what I could do to help.

"Jeff! Where are you?" I shouted.

The grizzly roared again right in Gwen's face. Her eyes rolled back and she collapsed in a dead faint.

Mr. McCarthy, still trapped inside his tent, hollered something, and I heard Jeff's rifle discharge from near the corral. The female bear turned away from Gwen and looked at me momentarily, then darted for the hanging elk. It growled and yanked down the carcass. Then, dragging the elk behind her and followed by the two yipping cubs, the grizzly disappeared into the darkness.

My lungs worked again. I looked at Gwen, heard Mr. McCarthy swearing, and wondered where Jeff was. My legs, however, would not work. Instead I found myself sliding down the station's wall into a seated position on the ground. Then I toppled over onto my side and joined Gwen in unconsciousness.

Chapter Twelve

My orders were clear that morning.

"Tonight," I said, "we sleep in the station. Y'all should start cleaning out those rooms after breakfast."

Jeff, holding a wet bandanna over a large welt on his forehead, slowly nodded. Gwen stared at me blankly. Mr. McCarthy just sighed.

I still had to gather up the livestock that had bolted during the bear raid, then repair the corral gate kicked open by a spooked animal. I shook my head and poured a cup of coffee. And then I started laughing.

Here I was, Raleigh Colter, a veteran frontiersman in the country I knew as well as most Apaches did. Yet I had passed out—fainted!—after a harrowing night with a mother bear and two cubs. Jeff Crutchfield, another respected guide, had tripped over a rock and knocked himself out, accidentally discharging his rifle, while running to help us. Mr. McCarthy spent the entire episode under a collapsed, heavy canvas tent before managing to crawl out and find everyone else unconscious.

My laugh must have been infectious because pretty soon Jeff and the McCarthys were grinning, then giggling, then boiling over with guffaws and back slapping. I was still chucking when I saddled up Dollie.

Well, it wasn't all funny. Because the bear had ripped one of my moccasins to pieces, I was forced to wear an extra pair of Stephen McCarthy's brogans. They were straight-last shoes in black leather and looked silly with my buckskin pants, and I felt silly wearing them. I was a moccasin man, though I did have a pair of boots back in my cabin that I wore at funerals and weddings. I reckon I should have been grateful, though, because it sure beat going around barefoot. And Mr. McCarthy had big feet, so at least those shoes didn't pinch me.

''Reckon I did wrong leaving that elk hanging from the tree,'' Crutchfield said as I shoved my rifle into the scabbard. That was obvious, I thought, and turned around to angrily agree with him. But one look at his hound-dog face, and I changed my tune. Besides, Jeff wasn't to blame.

''My fault,'' I said. ''I'm the leader of this group, and if anyone should know better than to leave fresh meat out in bear country, it's me.''

Crutchfield nodded. ''What was we thinkin'?''

I swung into the saddle and smiled. ''Jeff,'' I replied, ''we weren't.''

Rounding up the livestock took longer than I had expected. Dollie and Jeff's horse were the only animals that stayed close, and both returned to the corral before breakfast. But the McCarthys' mules and the scalphunters' horses lit a shuck for parts unknown. I found the packhorse in a canyon a few miles from camp, and the two saddle mounts I tracked up a heavily forested canyon to a creek. The mules, meanwhile, had run all the way to Delaware Springs—which had been the next station on the old Butterfield line—but at least they stayed on the road.

These animals I headed back up the trail to Guadalupe Pass, and herding mules and horses scared witless by bears is no easy chore. By the time I got back to the Pinery, it was late afternoon. I was dead tired and starving, but the sight I saw didn't help my appetite.

Six dead black-tailed rattlesnakes hung across the corral fence, and one of those serpents was as long as my leg and as wide as my calf. I had been right about snakes hibernating in the old buildings, but instead of feeling vindicated, I felt queasy. Jeff laughed when he saw me and knocked one of the snakes off the fence. It slithered eerily even though Jeff had shot its head off earlier in the day.

Some folks say a killed snake won't stop moving until after sundown.

One of the mules brayed anxiously, and I yelled. "These animals bolt again, Crutchfield, and you're rounding them up! Now get rid of those rattlers."

Laughing, Jeff found a canvas bag and put the dead snakes inside. "I swear, Colter, you're like a baby when it comes to snakes. Gwen killed one herself with a hoe."

Jeff Crutchfield and I had partnered together off and

on for many years now, but there were spells when I felt like shooting him. This was one of those times.

"Get rid of the snakes, Jeff!"

After driving the livestock into the corral, Jeff and I fixed the gate. The animals were fed, Jeff left to prepare supper, and I checked out the station. The McCarthys had taken to the task like my mother used to do every spring. This place would never be mistaken for The Drovers Cottage, but it looked inviting now.

Gwen and her father must have worked without stopping to get those rooms in order. Jeff probably helped a little, but I had my doubts if he did much other than kill snakes. A frontiersman like Crutchfield wouldn't soil his hands on housecleaning.

I inspected the rooms and was satisfied. No, I was pleased. They had already moved our bed gear inside, patched the holes in the roof, even cleaned up some rough-hewn furniture that had been abandoned. There was a stool and table in one room. The McCarthys took that room. Jeff and I would share a room with a boulder for a chair, while our supplies had been moved into the third room.

Gwen tossed me an old deerskin that had been left hanging on the walls.

"For making a moccasin," she suggested.

I stared at the massive brogans on my feet. "What? You don't like my new shoes?" My sarcasm was evident.

She just smiled.

*   *   *

We had black-tailed rattlesnake and coffee for supper. I think if Jeff Crutchfield had a choice between snake meat or a five-dollar dinner at a San Antonio hotel, he'd pick the snake meat. He wolfed down that awful food like he was gorging himself on scalloped oysters while the rest of us washed it down with plenty of coffee.

"Hardly what I would call palatable," Mr. McCarthy said.

I nodded. It didn't taste good, either.

But if supper wasn't so hot, at least our new sleeping accommodations were. Sometimes you sleep outside so much you forget just how good four walls and a roof can be. And while the wind howled outside, I was comfortable in my bedroll. Then Jeff Crutchfield started snoring.

Sleepily I stumbled out of the station at dawn and took a lungful of fresh, cold, mountain air. Crutchfield was still sawing logs as I went about my chores, again breaking the ice in the water trough for the livestock, stoking the fire, and putting the coffee on.

Breakfast was coffee, cold biscuits, and jerky. Not fancy, I assure you, but the McCarthys and I found it better than black-tailed rattlers. I figured I'd send Jeff out hunting for a mule deer or something later while I found a place for Gwen to set up her camera and hope for a mountain lion to show up. Now that we had the station cleaned out, we could store fresh game inside and not worry about a grizzly bear paying a midnight visit.

After breakfast Jeff volunteered to take Mr. Mc-Carthy hunting while I took Gwen in search of a mountain lion. We gathered around the "What-Is-It Wagon" to discuss our plans and decide what time we'd meet back in camp.

Gwen took a deep breath of cool air, exhaled, and looked please. "It's such a beautiful morning," she said, "and so quiet."

I suddenly knew something was wrong. Birds should have been singing and squirrels chattering. I had just turned around when an arrow slammed into the side of the wagon—only inches from my head.

Chapter Thirteen

I grabbed the Starr revolver as I spun around, and Jeff swung his Mississippi rifle to his shoulder. Another arrow landed between my borrowed brogans, and a gunshot exploded, its echoes bouncing off the mountains. Jeff groaned and dropped the rifle, its stock shattered by a heavy shell.

I froze, leaving my revolver in its sash, and glanced at Crutchfield. He stood motionless, staring numbly at two large splinters in the palm of his right hand and at his ruined rifle on the dirt at his feet.

Gwen and Stephen McCarthy were quiet. Too shocked, I figured. I was surprised too—at being alive. I silently cursed myself for not being more careful as a dozen Mescalero Apaches swarmed around us on foot, brandishing rifles, bows and arrows, and one long-bladed lance. But the fact that I was still breathing gave me faint hope, so I forced a wild smile and spread my arms out in a welcome gesture.

"Buenos días, mi hermanos," I tried. My Mescalero was far from passable, but Apaches usually understood Spanish. I thanked them for the visit, offered

them our coffee, and said that it was always good to see my Mescalero friends.

A young brave slammed me against the wagon and pressed a massive bone-handled knife against my throat, just pricking the skin so that I felt blood mixing with sweat. With his left hand, he tossed my revolver and bowie knife to the ground and grunted something.

More braves moved in, forcing Crutchfield and the McCarthys against the wagon with tightly drawn bow strings. In a matter of seconds, they would pin us all to the black wagon as a lesson for invading their country.

"What is the problem?" I asked in Spanish. "We have always camped in peace in these mountains." For the most part that was true, but these Apaches weren't sociable. The blade cut deeper into my throat and I decided to remain silent since my talking had gotten us nowhere—except maybe one breath from death.

Another brave shouted something in heavy, guttural Mescalero, and others responded excitedly. Then there was a long silence as a path cleared for man riding a fine, strong dun with dark legs, mane, and tail. The bridle and saddle were Army issue, but the rider was all Mescalero.

He wore a fringed buckskin shirt covered by a sutler's wool vest decorated with brass studs. Black and red beads covered his moccasins, and his buckskin leggings were well worn and stained. A plaid blanket was wrapped around his waist, and a buckskin war cap, heavily beaded, topped his head. He carried a medicine shield painted black in his left hand and held a Sharps rifle loosely in his right.

Long black hair fell across his shoulders, and the coldest black eyes I have ever seen bore a hole through me. His nose was Roman, his jaw firm, and a hard frown was chiseled into a solid, copper face streaked with black paint across his cheeks.

"Demonio," I whispered.

"What does that mean?" Gwen murmured, the first words she had spoken since the Apaches arrived.

Crutchfield answered for me: "It means we're dead."

Now newspapers spent a lot of ink on the likes of Cochise and Mangas Colorado, and later Victorio and Geronimo, but I think Demonio could have licked them all. No one knew his Apache name, so the Mexicans called him Demonio, meaning Demon, after his lightning-fast raids left herders, traders, and sometimes entire villages dead. He wasn't too popular north of the border, either, with his murders and horse stealing. The Texas governor had even offered a five-thousand-dollar reward for his head.

No one I knew had ever tried to collect.

There are two sides to every story, however, and a Mexican wolfer once told me that Demonio had been a peace-loving Mescalero until Mexican scalphunters raided his village and left his wife and children dead. An American Army officer had taken him prisoner during the '50s under a flag of truce, then hanged two other Mescalero captives after Demonio escaped. So I figured that he had a reason for carrying on a private war—not that it would do me any good.

Crutchfield was right. We were dead.

The Indian leader spoke something, quietly but firmly, and the brave lowered his knife from my throat and stepped away. After Demonio spoke again, the brave nodded and ran toward the corral. Then the other Mescaleros backed away from Crutchfield and the McCarthys and lowered their weapons. Mr. McCarthy sighed heavily, but I knew we were far from safe.

"Why do you come here?" Demonio asked in Spanish.

I stepped forward awkwardly, as if I stood before royalty—and in a way, I did—and replied, gesturing toward the McCarthys, "These visitors come from far away and wish to see these mountains. They wish . . ."

Words left me. How was I supposed to explain the photographic process to a Mescalero Apache who had never even seen a camera?

"How do you say magic in Spanish, Jeff?" I asked in a whisper.

"*Magia.*"

"She," I said, making a grand gesture toward Gwen, "has a magic box that captures . . . a vision . . ." I was struggling for words. "On paper. This magic . . . can be used to tell a story . . . much like the old Mescalero drawings in the caves at Hueco Tanks."

I had seen those strange paintings at the stagecoach

station south of here many times. Actually, one of those government scientists had told me some of that rock art dated farther back than the Apaches but a lot of it was Mescalero.

"Magic box?" Demonio asked in Spanish.

"*Sí.*"

There was an unmounted Apache at Demonio's side who I had not noticed before, a tall man with silver-streaked black hair and an open-topped fur turban decorated with eagle feathers and polished agate stones. A cougar skin hung around his neck. He carried no weapon, only a medicine shield crisscrossed with tin-cone pendants.

This man scoffed. I didn't have to understand Apache to realize he was telling Demonio that I was a liar. As the older man worked up steam, raising his voice and pointing angrily at me, I quickly looked at my Starr revolver, measuring its distance and my chances.

They were zero, of course, but I figured that maybe I could kill Demonio and cause the others to panic briefly. Then with luck, I could reverse aim and . . . I stopped. *I would not kill Gwen McCarthy.* Some Texicans believed that a woman was better off dead than living with Indians. Well, I figured that being alive is better than being dead any time. So I changed my plan and figured that I'd just try to kill Demonio and that medicine man before the rest of the Mescaleros finished me off. Who knows? Maybe Jeff and the McCarthys could escape during the confusion.

Angry shouts from the corral ended the conversation between Demonio and his lieutenant, and I turned my attention toward the brave who had pricked my throat. He led three horses toward the Mescalero leader and stopped a few yards from us, shouted something, and pointed an accusing finger in our direction. His face was contorted in rage, and his antics were working up the other Apaches.

I closed my eyes, understanding. The horses had belonged to the scalphunters. Apparently those men had also been successful butchering Mescaleros in addition to Mexicans, and these Indians recognized the horses and believed that we were the killers. One look from Demonio and I knew we were dead.

''Make a run for it when I go for my gun,'' I told Crutchfield, and was about to dive for the Starr when Gwen jumped forward, kicking my gun across the camp and yelling, ''No!''

Chapter Fourteen

Gwen ran toward Demonio, but a warrior—just a boy, really—threatened her with a lance. Before the rest of us could move, the other braves raised their weapons. Someone shouted. Mr. McCarthy gasped in terror. Gwen backed away from the lance but kept her eyes locked on the Mescalero leader.

She read the scene exactly as I did—the Apaches thought we were scalphunters—and shouted furiously at Demonio and his lieutenant. Of course, she was speaking English, and the Apaches' faces were expressionless. She took a deep breath, tried to regain some semblance of composure, and spoke again, calmer now and using her hands in a novice sign language.

"This man," she said and pointed to me, "Colter. He killed"—here she struck a finger across her throat—"the men you hunt. That is why we have their horses."

Demonio's face yielded no emotion.

Gwen pulled her hair in exasperation. "Don't you understand?" She quickly turned to me. "Colter! Show him your arm." I obliged, pulling up a tattered shirtsleeve to reveal my bandaged bullet wound. "See! This man Colter was shot while he killed your enemies."

I cleared my throat and took a couple of cautious steps forward. My guard tightened his grip on his bowstring, but I took a deep breath. Every pair of Apache eyes locked on me now—except Demonio, who continued to stare at Gwen.

"The men you seek are dead," I said in Spanish. "I killed them in the desert south of here. Your enemies are my enemies."

No one spoke for several minutes. I wasn't even sure Demonio had heard, but then he spoke without taking his eyes off Gwen.

"And the parts of my people?"

He meant the scalps. "I found no Mescalero scalps," I said. "Only those of Mexicans, disguised to look like those of *Indeh.*" Here I used the Apache word for Apache, which meant "The People." "These I buried away from our enemies."

Yeah, I was stumping but not lying. You didn't lie to an Apache like Demonio. He would know. Then he would kill you.

Now Demonio turned and looked me in the eye. "It is known," he said, "that our enemies the Mexicans will pay much money that you men cherish for the hair of *Indeh.* Why would a white man throw away such treasure?"

I chose my words carefully. "It is known that *Indeh* do not scalp their enemies. I am like you. I do not believe in the practice. It is wrong."

"It is true," Demonio said. "Now we shall see if you speak truthfully." He shouted something in Mescalero and Gwen and I were forced back against the wagon with Jeff and Mr. McCarthy. Apache chatter intensified for a few minutes after Demonio barked out another order, and then an eerie quietness enveloped the camp as an ancient figure slowly stepped forward.

She wore buckskins and a blanket over her head as she shuffled her feet, eyes downcast, and made her way toward us. She was an elderly woman, her face a prune of deep wrinkles, who had been beaten savagely. Her right eye was swollen shut and there was a deep slash across her right hand. When she stood only a few feet from us and looked up, I knew why she wore the blanket over her head. She had been scalped and left for dead.

Her eyes studied me intently, then Crutchfield and Mr. McCarthy. She did not bother to look at Gwen but examined the horses instead. Slowly she walked to Demonio, looked up, and muttered something in Mescalero.

The Indian beside Demonio frowned and protested, other Mescaleros joined in, but Demonio raised his right hand slightly and all were silent. After a few brief, maybe even kind, words from Demonio, the woman shuffled her way back.

"She says you are not the ones who took her hair," Demonio told me. "But she recognized the horses."

I nodded, feeling vindicated. "It is as I have spoken. Your enemies were killed by me."

Demonio shook his head. "Five men raided our camp while our men were hunting. You have spoken that you killed two men. Perhaps you are the other three."

He raised his voice and several braves took off running, some to the station rooms and another climbed into the back of the wagon. Demonio's lieutenant looked at me and grinned. "Magic box," he said, then snickered. "Soon you will die."

It made sense, of course. The scalphunters had raided the Mescalero camp, then split up. The two men that I had killed must have murdered some Mexicans shortly after and were headed to the rendezvous site when they attacked Gwen and me. Later we learned that the three other scalphunters were shot dead when they tried to rob a bank in Mesilla, New Mexico Territory. 'Course, right then it didn't really matter. I knew the Apaches wouldn't find any Mescalero scalps, but that wouldn't stop them from killing us. They thought we were the killers, and with us having the incriminating horses, I couldn't really blame them.

"Why?" I whispered to Gwen. "Why did you kick my revolver away? It was our only chance."

"I followed your advice. I read his eyes. They're honest, like yours."

Shaking my head, I looked first at Demonio, then at Gwen. That woman was wrongheaded as all get-out. My eyes were blue; the Apache's were darker than gunpowder and twice as explosive, and his face lacked any emotion. I sighed. My head ached. I wished

I had left the McCarthys and Jeff Crutchfield alone back at Rodolpho's.

"Aiiyeeeeee!"

The scream came from the wagon, and a young brave dashed out and shoved two pieces of paper at Demonio. For once, the Mescalero looked shocked. His lieutenant grabbed the papers and tossed them down, stumbling in fear. Others gathered around the items but quickly backed away.

Quickly Demonio slid from his saddle, tossing his rifle to one brave and his shield to another. He picked up the papers and hurriedly approached me, shoving two photographic prints in my face.

"Explain!" he shouted. "Tell me!"

There I was, in black and white, standing in front of the medicine mounds that the Apaches worshipped. And in the other picture stood Jeff Crutchfield, though slightly blurry. I withheld a smile and took back everything I had said to myself about the McCarthys.

"Magia." I said. I pointed to Gwen. "I told you about her magic box. She has the power to capture you on paper."

Demonio backed away, his focus now on Gwen. "Show me," he said, his voice barely audible, "this magic box."

The Apaches distanced themselves from Gwen as she pulled out her camera and supplies. She tried explaining the photographic process to the Indians, partly in signs, partly with me translating into Spanish, but they looked at her in fear. I'm not sure they would have been as in awe if the photographs had not been taken at the medicine mounds. That added to their superstitions.

"I need a subject," Gwen said, looking at Demonio.

"No," Demonio said. "I won't have my soul captured on white man's magic paper. It will steal my shadow."

I showed the leader my shadow, but he wouldn't change his opinion. Nor would his lieutenant. Finally a boy stepped forward, smiling broadly, and sat on a boulder in front of the camera.

A red silk headband was tied across his forehead, and long black hair fell almost a foot past his shoulders. He was shirtless but wore calf-high moccasins and a buckskin breechcloth. Covering his throat was a pendant made of tin cones, and braided horsehair bands were strapped to both wrists. He held a Colt Dragoon—the one I had given Crutchfield—in both hands and stared nervously at Gwen and her magic box.

"Be very still," Gwen said as she covered her head with the black cloth hanging behind her camera. I repeated the order to the Mescalero boy in Spanish. And then I murmured to Gwen: "Our lives are riding on this photograph."

"Don't worry, Colter," she said coolly.

She took the photograph, removed the plate, and disappeared into the back of her wagon, leaving the rest of us nervously facing Demonio and his men. It seemed as if Gwen were in there for hours. Finally, she reappeared. I tried to exhale as Gwen smiled and walked over to the Mescalero boy and offered him the photograph.

The boy's toothy smile was gone. He backed up a little, but Gwen closed the gap. ''Here,'' she said. ''Take it.'' His eyes were tightly shut and he stood rigid, but Gwen's voice was soothing, even if he couldn't understand her words. ''It's all right, son. It won't hurt you. Look.''

After several seconds, the boy finally opened his eyes and saw the print. Suddenly he snatched it from Gwen's hands and turned to face his people. He threw his head back and let go a blood-curdling ''Aii-yeeeeee!''

Chapter Fifteen

First the boy dashed into the sunlight and looked at the ground. Satisfied that Gwen's "magic" had not robbed him of his shadow, he sprinted to his friends and showed them the photograph. The Mescaleros gathered around him and muttered excitedly. Demonio spoke, and the chatter stopped immediately. With his head down, the boy nervously walked to the Apache leader and handed him the photograph.

Demonio studied the picture, then handed it back to the boy, who hurried back to his friends. Followed closely by his lieutenant, Demonio walked to the big camera and studied it. Cautiously he felt the black cloth. Next he squatted and examined the tripod.

"It is a three-legged beast!" the lieutenant shouted in Spanish, then lashed out something in Mescalero. From the little Apache I understood, I guessed that he was telling Demonio they should destroy this monster before Ussen, the Apache god, destroyed them.

But Demonio rose, shaking his head, and pointed to Gwen. First he spoke in Mescalero, then translated into Spanish: "The woman controls this magic box. It did not rob——" (the boy's Mescalero name was lost

92

on me) "of his shadow. It is not an evil magic box. A person with the power of this magic box would have no need of killing *Indeh*. I believe these people speak the truth."

I let go a sigh that was probably heard in Franklin. The Apaches lowered their weapons, and many rushed forward to touch Gwen and her camera. Demonio's lieutenant grumbled something and stormed angrily away. I walked to Demonio and did some more stumping: "I am thankful that the great Demonio has seen the truth of my words. I have never considered the Mescaleros my enemies. My camp is your camp. Welcome."

He nodded curtly and walked away, leaving me disappointed. I had hoped to talk to him some more. Few white men had lived after seeing Demonio, but he mounted his horse and disappeared. The rest of the Apaches stayed awhile, however. Fact is, we had a regular party all morning.

Gwen took three more photographs and made prints for her subjects: a teenage girl, a mother and her infant, and a young brave. They paid her for the prints, of course. The Indians wouldn't have it any other way, so Gwen came away with a tin-cone pendant, awl, clay pot, and bone choker.

Jeff and Mr. McCarthy mingled with some braves and did some trading of their own. The Army would frown upon the fact that Crutchfield let the Mescaleros take some rifles and revolvers, but at least Jeff wouldn't part with the best weapons: the Henry and

Yellow Boy rifles. Me? I met with an elderly man who took an interest in the brogans on my feet. After some haggling—with Stephen McCarthy's blessing—I traded the ill-fitting brogans for a pair of calf-high, slightly beaded moccasins. They fit me perfectly, and although the leather shoes were too big for the Mescalero, he wore them proudly.

Finally Demonio and his lieutenant returned. The warrior spoke, and his subjects gathered their belongings.

The scalphunters' horses were loose grazing where the Apaches had left them, so I grabbed the hackamores and pulled the animals behind me as I walked to Demonio.

"These," I said, "I present as a gift to the woman who was wronged by our enemies."

Demonio nodded, and a brave gathered the horses and hurried away. Demonio's eyes moved, and I realized Gwen was at my side.

"This," he asked, "is your woman?"

Now I was at a dilemma. I couldn't lie to Demonio. But if Demonio wanted to take her for a bride, well . . . Gwen looked at me, uncomprehending. "He wants to know if you're my woman," I whispered. "I think he would like to marry you."

"Oh, my."

Clearing my throat, I tried to stand tall and straight. "I . . ." Gwen McCarthy was mule-headed. She had picked fights with me, offended me, embarrassed me, almost gotten me killed. Yet right then I realized that

I had feelings for her. My eyes locked on Demonio's, and I continued: "She is not my woman, but I would like her to be. And I would fight to keep her, even if it meant fighting the great Demonio."

I swear but I believe Demonio smiled—ever so briefly, but a smile nonetheless. "She is worth fighting for," he said. His expression turned serious and he added: "White man, I leave you in peace. You have fought my enemies, and that is good. Your woman has powerful magic, and that also is good. These mountains are our home, but I cannot guarantee your safety once we are gone. Others may come, *Indeh* or enemies. They may kill you."

"I understand."

Demonio kicked his horse's ribs and trotted away, followed by his people. They crossed the road, turned south, and vanished into the vast countryside as quickly as they had appeared. When they were gone, Gwen looked at me and asked, "What did you tell him? About us?"

I was so used to talking to the Mescaleros that I almost replied in Spanish. Grinning, I lied, "We're working on a trade. I'm trying to get the price up."

Her kick was well placed, and I yelped and grabbed my left shin, hopped a couple of times, and fell to the ground in pain.

We ate corn and sun-dried mescal cakes traded by the Apaches, then got back to business. Gwen loaded her camera and supplies on the pack mule and threw a sidesaddle on another mule. I saddled Dollie and off we went in search of a mountain lion, leaving Jeff and Mr. McCarthy resting up in camp for a hunting trip later in the day.

I headed northwest to a spring that attracted mule deer, elk, and other game, figuring that a hungry puma might decide to hunt there before dusk. Gwen set up her camera in a grove of trees so that we would be well hidden, and I staked our animals several hundred yards away but kept them in view. The last thing I wanted was a mountain lion to make a meal out of Dollie or Gwen's mules. I took the Henry rifle and made myself comfortable near Gwen.

Now we waited.

"What do you think our chances are?" Gwen asked.

I was cleaning my Starr, which had gotten sand in its mechanisms when Gwen kicked it across the camp yard that morning. Gwen's chances of taking a decent photograph of a lion were zero, but I shrugged. "If we don't see anything today, tomorrow we'll go higher into the mountains. Hunting a lion is hard enough, but you have to carry that giant camera around. That won't be easy in rough country."

"I thought you didn't *hunt* mountain lions."

"Not for sport."

"I see."

Well, I could tell by her tone that she didn't see, so I explained: "A mountain lion killed one of my horses back at my cabin a couple of years ago. I tracked him down and killed him because I didn't want him coming back and killing any more of my animals. That's different than killing an animal for a trophy or something. I mean, it's not like hunting wolves.''

"I see," she repeated. Now, I've been called a lot of vile names before, but I don't think anything said to me was as annoying as those two words. Gwen used them like some folks would a knife. "You've hunted wolves?" she asked.

"Hunted. Trapped. Poisoned. Coyotes are a nuisance, but wolves are evil. Ought to exterminate them all.'' I cocked my Starr, satisfied that it was in perfect order, and shoved it into my sash, then dug out some chewing tobacco. '' 'Course,'' I reflected, ''the bounties are enticing.''

"Bounties? You shoot them for money?"

I worked a good plug in my cheek and nodded, pointing to my hat. "Bought this hat for three wolf pelts," I admitted.

Gwen laughed. "You're a man of contradictions, Colter. You adamantly refused to guide us when you thought we were hunting a mountain lion to kill, but you'll shoot—poison even—wolves for money.''

I sent a stream of brown juice splashing against a rock. "Wolves are different.''

"They're all God's creatures.''

My face reddened, and I sat up thinking that I should have let Demonio take this woman out of my hair. "Look," I argued, "you own some land or livestock around these parts and you'll sing a different tune. You ever see what a pack of wolves can do to a horse, or cattle, or sheep? It ain't pretty.''

''Um. I see.''

She might as well have shot me. Groaning, I pulled my hat down over my head and leaned back, exasperated. Gwen never brought up wolves or hunting again, however, and I figured that I had convinced her my thinking was right. That is, until I sat down to write this memoir. And then I realized that I have never trapped, poisoned, or hunted a wolf—or coyote, or mountain lion—since that day.

Chapter Sixteen

No mountain lion showed up, but Gwen took a photograph of an elk drinking at the springs. She wasn't optimistic about the print turning out because of the fading light, however, so I fetched the animals and we returned to camp around dusk. After rubbing down the animals in the corral, I nodded toward El Capitán and told Gwen that we'd take off for the high country at first light.

The camp was empty, so I got a fire going and put some coffee on. I was chewing on jerky to tide me over till supper when a horse whinnied. My right hand instinctively found the butt of my Starr, but I was certain it was Crutchfield, and sure enough he rounded the corner on his horse. I immediately noticed the small mule deer strapped behind his saddle and smiled with satisfaction. Venison was a tad better than rattlesnake. Then I noticed something else.

"Where's Mr. McCarthy?" I asked.

Crutchfield's face registered surprise as he dropped from his saddle. "The old man? Ain't he here?"

Worry gnawed at the pit of my stomach. "No," I replied. "You two were going hunting."

"Yeah, but Mr. McCarthy decided to stay here. Said he was tuckered out. Maybe he just wandered out to nature's call or went for a walk. He's prone to walking."

Yeah, I thought, but leisurely strolls weren't recommended in this country. Not alone. Gwen walked over then and knew something was wrong. "Where's Father?" she asked tentatively.

Light was fading fast, so I tried to pick up a trail. That wasn't easy to do because of all the Apache tracks, but finally I read a trail made by brogans headed toward El Capitán and Guadalupe Peak. Maybe he had just gone for a walk, but he should have been back by now. Anyone, but especially a greenhorn, could get lost in these mountains.

"We'll find him," I assured Gwen as I saddled Dollie. But I wasn't convinced. Gwen demanded that she accompany me, and I relented, leaving Jeff at camp with orders to fire three shots in the air if Mr. McCarthy returned. I'd fire two shots if we found him all right, two shots followed by three more if I needed help.

Cold wind bit through our clothes, but Gwen and I moved on slowly higher into the mountains. His trail would be blown away in a matter of hours, and darkness would make tracking him difficult, if not impossible, but I worked with grim determination, studying the sign.

He sat on a dead log for a long while, then walked

on for a few hundred yards before resting again. This was easy enough to read, and expected. Stephen McCarthy wasn't used to the high altitude, so he had to stop often to catch his breath. He had rested on a boulder before moving on. He was stumbling now, really tired, I thought, but then my eyes caught something glinting beneath a juniper tree.

I dropped to the ground and crawled under the tree. My right hand clasped a bottle and I sighed as I walked to Gwen. The cork was gone but a finger of golden liquid remained in the bottle, and I recognized the smell immediately. Apparently, Stephen McCarthy had done some serious trading on his own with the Mescaleros. Then he had stayed behind at camp to go on a high lonesome.

''Tequila,'' I said heavily and tossed the bottle away.

An hour later, tracking became pointless. His trail had vanished in the wind, which felt like ice in the darkness. But Gwen refused to return to camp, so we rode on, screaming out McCarthy's name and listening above the wind's howls and the din of yipping coyotes and wolves.

Finally, the cold was too much for us, so I found a natural amphitheater in a mountainside and pulled a shivering Gwen McCarthy from her sidesaddle. I gathered some dry twigs and brush and found the flint, steel, and charred cloth I kept in a small tinderbox. Striking the sharp flint against the steel, I soon had the cloth glowing. I placed tinder around it and began blowing steadily until the fire was going.

Gwen's pack mule and Dollie were picketed in front of the depression, blocking the wind, and the fire soon warmed the mountain walls. I covered Gwen with my coat and chewed on jerky, trying to ignore the fact that I could have been eating roasted mule deer in the comfort of the Pinery Station if not for Stephen McCarthy.

Dollie snorted and threw her ears back, and I raised the Henry rifle and listened. A cougar growled in the night, and I rose and walked into the wind. My luck! I couldn't find a mountain lion for Gwen when I needed to, but now . . . Mountain lions are shy animals, really, so when the cat growled again I sent a bullet in its direction, the gunshot echoing across the mountains.

The mule jumped and brayed at the gunshot, but I patted her and scratched her ears, then made my way back to the comfort of the fire. I never heard the mountain lion again.

''He's dead, isn't he?'' The gunshot had awakened Gwen, and at first I didn't understand who she meant.

''My father. He's dead.''

I sat the rifle down and moved closer to her. She blinked away tears and tried to stop the flow but couldn't, and soon she was crying on my shoulder, mumbling that it was all her fault, that her father was dead, that they should have stayed in Boston. This was new to me. I didn't know what I was supposed to do, but I stroked her hair softly and held her close, telling her that everything was all right, that we would find her father safe and sound, that she shouldn't worry.

I kept this up until she was asleep, and then I tried to make myself comfortable without waking the sleeping beauty now on my lap. And soon I too drifted off to sleep, wondering if we would find Gwen's father alive the next morning or just his corpse.

We were up and moving at first light, skipping breakfast and ignoring the growling from our stomachs. Higher we went into the mountains, and I was about to turn back, figuring that Stephen McCarthy had not made it this far, when I noticed a piece of gray cotton hanging on the spines of a desert spoon plant.

Higher we moved until the trail became impassable. Gwen shouted for her father and the words echoed and faded away. Overhead a golden eagle screeched, and I noticed the giant nest built in the mountainside hundreds of feet above. It would have made a beautiful photograph, I thought.

The wind howled furiously this high up, and I studied the trail. It would have been hard for me to climb over these rocks and continue ascending the mountain, so I knew Stephen McCarthy had not gone farther. I walked back to Dollie and Gwen and had to shout to be heard over the wind: ''He couldn't have gone farther! We'll turn back and look some more!''

Gwen nodded. The eagle sounded again. And then

there was something else, a faint cry carried by the wind, barely audible. I listened closely, heard the cry again, and moved cautiously to the edge of the mountain. Tightening the latigo string on my hat because of the furious wind, I dropped to my stomach and inched my way forward until I was peering over the mountainside.

It was a drop of more than five hundred feet. I sucked in a lungful of air and swallowed. Maybe thirty feet below was Stephen McCarthy, clutching the branch of a small juniper growing on the mountainside with both hands.

I moved quickly now. ''Stay away from the edge!'' I ordered Gwen after telling her that her father was below. The wind could easily blow her over—that's what I figured happened to Mr. McCarthy. I grabbed my lariat and tied it to a boulder near the cliff, then slowly descended toward McCarthy. When I was only a few feet from him, I held the rope tightly with my left hand and reached out with my right.

''Grab my hand!'' I cried.

Just then the juniper branch snapped.

Chapter Seventeen

He dropped another ten feet, landing on a narrow limestone ledge that jutted out from the mountainside no more than a yard. McCarthy scrambled a bit and screamed when part of the ledge gave way and sent his left leg dangling.

"Don't move!" I cried, and the old man froze, his face ashen, knuckles white.

My rope was seventy feet long so I could still reach him, but I realized pulling him up would be a deadly chore. The ledge would not support both of us. Mr. McCarthy would have to save himself. I looked up, studying the cliff face in front of me. Time was my enemy. I wasn't sure how much longer the ledge would hold Gwen's father. My left hand tentatively let go of the reata and found a firm hold in the rock face. Careful not to look down, I poked the mountainside with my new moccasins and wedged my feet into narrow holes. Finally my right hand grasped a rock and I hugged the wall for dear life, pressing my face against the limestone and barely breathing.

"Gwen!" I yelled.

She quickly answered and I ordered: "Tie the reata

to the saddle horn on Dollie. When I tell you, pull her away from the side. We're going to bring us up one at a time, your father first. Hurry!''

Gwen was already moving. I felt the rope jerk up, opened my eyes, and saw it dancing in the wind to my side.

''It's ready, Colter!''

My right hand inched toward the reata, but the wind picked up and I groaned as the rope was carried farther away. Out stretched my arm until I had to stop to get a better hold on the cliff face with my left hand. My right foot suddenly slipped, causing my heart to skip, but quickly I found another foothold.

I kissed the side of the mountain and said a brief prayer.

The wind stopped and the rope swung back toward me. I opened my fist and just as the wind started again my hand grasped the hemp reata and pulled it close.

A full minute passed before I could move again. Slowly I looked down. The bottom ground seemed to rush up toward me and a wave of dizziness and nausea took my breath away and forced me to look up until the spell passed.

''McCarthy!'' I shouted after another minute. His answer was a timid whine. ''I'm going to swing the rope to you. Grab it and tie it around your waist. Make it tight.''

My right hand dropped and I began to swing the rope. Again I looked down, but this time I made sure I focused only on the trapped Easterner. The reata went right past him but he refused to move. One hand held the ledge and the other gripped the mountainside. He was too petrified to let go.

"Grab the rope!" I barked, and when he failed to respond I cursed him until I was out of breath. "Grab the rope, you fool!" I added. "Or both of us will die! Grab it!"

Finally his right hand reached out. He missed the rope the first time but seized it on the next pass. I sighed and watched as he awkwardly tied the rope around his waist, then gripped the rope with both hands.

"Now!" I shouted. "Pull him up, Gwen!"

Mr. McCarthy screamed as he was jerked forward just as the rest of the ledge crumbled and collapsed, falling silently to the ground hundreds of feet below. He swung below me and was slowly hoisted to safety, his eyes glued shut and his mouth moving silently in prayer. I moved cautiously out of his way as Dollie pulled him forward, finding other handholds and footholds. Then I made the mistake of looking up, only to have gravel and dust burn my eyes. I groaned and hugged the mountainside again.

"Lower the rope. Lower the rope. Lower the rope. Hurry." My voice was barely a whisper. Every muscle ached, and my fingers grew numb and weak. I couldn't hold on much longer. After blinking the dirt out of my eyes, I looked up. The rope was being lowered, now just a foot from me. I breathed deeply and felt both footholds giving way.

Quickly I reached out—almost jumping—and grabbed the reata with my right hand as my feet slipped and dangled. I bounced against the mountainside twice, then slid, the rope burning my hand, but my left hand grasped the reata and despite pain, I took hold of the rope and wrapped it around both hands.

"Pull!" I shouted, but I was already moving.

I didn't breathe again until I was on the trail.

Minutes passed before I could sit up, and my chest heaved. Gwen knelt beside me, and finally her voice registered: "Colter. Are you all right?"

Slowly I nodded, and she embraced me. My arms finally responded and hugged her tightly. My face collapsed against her shoulder and I deeply inhaled the smell of her hair. Then I pulled myself away and found my feet. There remained a lot to do.

Mr. McCarthy was freezing from exposure, so I built a fire and sat him close to it, then fired two shots in the air to let Crutchfield know we had found him. 'Course, I wasn't sure Jeff would be able to hear the shots, but I didn't want to move back to camp until Gwen's father was warmer.

He had spent all night in the freezing wind, sleeping under the rocks where the trail ended. That morning he somehow stumbled over the edge, miraculously grabbing the juniper branch and holding on for an hour, maybe more, until we arrived.

"I must have gotten lost," he said when the fire finally warmed his bones. "I just went for a walk and—"

"I found the bottle of tequila, McCarthy." My tone was far from friendly.

He looked at me, and slowly his eyes found his daughter. Tears welled, and finally he burst out crying, pleading to God for another chance, vowing that he would never drink again, that he didn't want to die. He buried his face in his hands, but Gwen moved over and comforted him. I left them alone, partly to get ready to return to the station but mostly to give them privacy.

And when I looked into Stephen McCarthy's face after I returned, I believed that he had finally beaten his demons and that he would never touch John Barleycorn again.

We took it slow coming down the mountain. With the McCarthys riding double on their mule and with the old man still weak, there was no cause to hurry. Jeff smiled when he rode into camp, and Gwen led her father to their room in the station. Stephen McCarthy was worn out, half dead. He would sleep most of the day.

"Got to admit," Crutchfield said as I watered and fed the animals, "that I was gettin' a tad worried."

"You hear my shots?"

"Heard somethin' last night, but just one shot. Didn't hear nothin' today."

I soaked my rope-burned right hand in the water trough, then examined it. Crutchfield frowned.

"What happened to you?"

I shook my head.

"Well, where did you find Mr. McCarthy?"

After a heavy sigh, I replied, "Jeff, you don't want to know." Stephen McCarthy wasn't the only one tuckered out. I found my bedroll in the station and immediately fell asleep.

It was dusk when I woke up. Gwen held my right hand in hers and was gently applying salve to the rope burn. My entire body ached, but her touch was gentle. She smiled and wrapped my hand in a makeshift bandage.

Our eyes met. "Thank you," she said softly. "Thank you, Raleigh, for saving my father."

Her voice was like an angel's. I even liked the way she said "Raleigh." I shrugged. "It's what I'm getting paid for."

"No, it's not." And she leaned over and kissed my forehead, brushed my hair back, and stood to go. "You need some more sleep."

She was almost out of the room when I called her name. Gwen turned around, a silhouette in the door frame.

"You know what?" I asked.

"What?"

"I think this is the first day that's gone by that we haven't had a fight."

Her laughter was like music as she walked away. Smiling, I rolled over and went back to sleep.

Chapter Eighteen

A bitter cold front blew in the following night, but the weather did not dampen Gwen's resolve. She was determined to capture a mountain lion on film even if it meant scouring every mountain and canyon in the Guadalupe range. 'Course, I wasn't really complaining. Truth is, I enjoyed her company.

We staked out water holes where deer were plentiful. We took to the high country, Gwen lugging that forty-pound camera over boulders and through thick juniper. We even peered into dark caves. We did not, however, see any sign of the animal.

"I'm really disappointed in you, Colter," Gwen chided me over supper. "Back at Borachio Station everyone said you were the only man for the job. And so far, I've seen nothing."

"Oh, you can't say that, Gwen," Mr. McCarthy cut in. "We've seen grizzly bears, rattlesnakes, and Mescaleros thanks to Mr. Colter."

He chuckled and soon had Crutchfield and Gwen laughing with him—at my expense. I liked the old man better when he was a drunk, I said to myself, but a smile soon appeared on my face too.

"We'll find one," I said confidently. "We'll get an early start tomorrow, hit the southern range."

Mountain lions really aren't aggressive. They avoid humans and rarely attack livestock. They are beautiful animals, strong, lean, and graceful. I'd take their company over an ornery old housecat any day. But I knew why we were having trouble seeing a lion.

Gwen made a lot of noise hauling her camera, and it was slow going, especially in rough country. By the time we made much distance, any mountain lion that had been nearby would have hightailed it away from all the racket we were making.

I devised a new strategy as I worked an after-supper plug of tobacco into my cheek. I'd become a hunter and track a mountain lion much as I had done with the one that killed my horse. After finding the trail, I would pursue the animal awhile, then have Gwen set up her camera, and I'd chase the animal back toward her. When the lion saw Gwen it would freeze and growl, Gwen could take her photo, then I'd fire a shot to scare the puma away.

Yes, it was a long shot. Yes, there was an element of danger, but I doubted if a mountain lion would attack Gwen. That huge black camera had scared fearless Mescalero Apaches; it would certainly do the same to a timid cougar.

Well, it wasn't the best idea I ever had—but time was getting short. It was November, and I didn't want to get snowed in up here.

* * *

We traveled south to the edge of the Guadalupe range, then moved up through hard terrain. When the trail became impassable, I hobbled Dollie and Gwen's mules and left them, hauling ropes, Winchester, and canteen and some of Gwen's gear. She wouldn't trust me with the camera, though, even when she had to climb over loose gravel and up steep inclines.

At one point I had to rope a rock twenty-five feet above and climb up, then hoist our supplies. Gwen had no choice. This time she had to let me pull up her camera. Next I had to lift her. I dropped neither.

We caught our breath, fighting the altitude and thin air. I offered Gwen a piece of jerky and she washed it down with water, staring at the vast nothingness that stretched seemingly forever, a stark whiteness four thousand feet below.

"Salt Flats," I said. "You can see the dry salt lakes over there."

"Peaceful looking," Gwen observed.

A few years later, those flats wouldn't be so peaceful. They would be the center point of a bloody feud that eventually would bring in the Texas Rangers. I never really thought of the flats as "peaceful looking," though, mainly because as a stagecoach driver I hated whipping my team across that dry expanse. By the time I reached the station at Ojos de los Alamos, I was covered from hat to moccasin with gray-white sand.

"I can see why you come here," Gwen said, "why you love this place."

"Not here," I said. "But I'll show you a special place sometime. The most beautiful canyon I've ever seen."

"I look forward to it."

We were having a wonderful conversation until something commanded my attention and I excitedly ran to a boulder and knelt. Mountain lion droppings! I reached down and picked up a piece, broke it open and rubbed it with my fingers.

I wiped my hand on my buckskin pants, unable to conceal my excitement. When I looked for Gwen, however, I was surprised to see her mouth wide open in astonishment. Maybe *stunned* would be a better word.

"Colter!" She finally found her voice. "I can't believe what I just saw! I hope you're going to wash your hands—now!"

"It's called tracking," I told Gwen. "That scat is less than a day old and is the first sign we've seen. I bet we see a lion today."

"After you wash your hands!"

I wasted good canteen water to pacify Gwen, scoured my fingers with dirt, and brushed them off on my shirttail. We moved quickly, and when I pointed out fresh puma tracks an hour later, Gwen forgot all about my lack of Boston house manners. I knew we were getting closer, and my heart pounded. The trail ran into another dead end, but I climbed over several rocks and pulled myself up the final ten yards. I lowered the rope and again slowly brought up the camera and other gear. Gwen struggled over the rocks, insisting that she climb all the way, although she finally relented and let me pull her up the last five feet.

"You did well," I said, and I meant it.

She tried to catch her breath, unable to respond, so we waited.

"Look at that," she finally said and pointed excitedly toward the east. I studied the view but saw only the distant Delaware Mountains and Brushy Mesa—just more rocks and high desert.

"The lighting is spectacular. Oh, Colter, I must take a picture of this. It's beautiful."

I shrugged. "Suit yourself," and pulled out my tobacco pouch while Gwen set up her camera.

Gwen pointed the lens at the overlook and ducked beneath her black cloth, and I tried to see what made this scene such a wonderful opportunity. She was talking about depth of field, contrast, and shadows, stuff that never made sense to me. Then again, I'd probably bore her to tears talking about powder loads, trajectories, and caliber.

She slid a glass plate into the box, studied her subject once more, and said softly, "Here goes."

Right then, we heard the distinct growl behind us.

I wheeled and looked, and Gwen turned and gasped. Forty feet away from us sat a female mountain lion. She was sitting on her back legs, ears straight up, massive tail motionless. Her coat was reddish brown, and she was probably six feet long, weighing one hundred and eighty pounds. The Winchester was at my feet, but that cat could cover the distance between us in two bounds. She'd be on top of me before I ever got the rifle cocked.

I knew mountain lions were timid and figured this one would run away if I made some noise. Then again, there was always the chance that this one was rabid, fearless, hungry, or ornery.

Slowly I pulled the Starr revolver from my sash, though I wasn't sure if a pistol bullet would stop that cat. The mountain lion took a step toward us. I froze. The puma's tail moved like a snake behind her. She growled again but suddenly sprinted away from us, leaping over an avalanche of boulders and disappearing.

I exhaled and looked at Gwen. First she glanced at me, then at her camera, still pointing in the opposite direction of the mountain lion, and finally at her panoramic subject. We knew we'd never get a chance like this again—even if we lived to be a hundred.

"Colter," she said softly, "shoot me."

Chapter Nineteen

After Gwen took her scenic photograph, I lost the mountain lion's trail in the rocks, so we returned to camp—with me expecting to bring Gwen back to the mountain the next day since we knew that cat's territory. Mountain lions have a limited hunting range in the winter, and I figured the cat had staked out no more than ten square miles for herself.

The cold front had moved out by the following morning, and Gwen suggested we take a one-day vacation from puma hunting. I nodded in agreement, remembering climbing rocks and pulling up gear with a rope. Jeff had ridden out before dawn to scout the roads and check for Indian sign. He returned while Gwen and I were discussing our options, hung a haversack on one of the station's log rafters, and poured a cup of coffee.

"Why don't y'all go on a picnic," Mr. McCarthy suggested, and his daughter's eyes brightened.

"Yes," she said, "you can show me that canyon you were bragging about."

I liked the idea. We could pack some venison sandwiches, spend the whole day together—alone.

"Jeff, would like to come with us?" Gwen asked.

"Sounds great," Crutchfield replied and nodded at his haversack. "I killed a rattler in the desert this morn'. We could fry her up for dinner."

"Jeff," Stephen McCarthy said, "I thought perhaps we could go hunting today. You said you'd let me try to bag an elk."

"Huh?"

"I'd really like to go hunting today. Let Gwen and Colter have their picnic. We'll do some real hunting."

Crutchfield stared at me. Finally he grinned. Jeff was slow at times, but he wasn't a simpleton. "That sounds like a fine idea," he said. "We'll save the rattlesnake for supper."

Mr. McCarthy grumbled something, and I headed for the corral. "Let me bring my camera!" Gwen called out, but I responded with a firm no.

"This is a picnic, remember? No camera for you."

We rode northeast along the Butterfield Road for a few miles, then turned west along a white-walled canyon and traveled a couple of miles before reining to a halt. I picketed Dollie and Gwen's mule in a grove of trees while Gwen got the sack carrying our dinner.

"What's this?" she asked, pointing to a circle of stones in the dirt.

"Roasting pit," I replied. "Mescaleros will use hot stones to roast mescal crowns for food, like those cakes we got from Demonio's people."

She bent over and picked up something shining in

the dirt. It was a brass cartridge, unfired, and a big shell. "Fifty-six caliber," I said. "Spencer rifle. Not like an Apache to be so careless with ammunition."

Gwen smiled. "A present for you."

I shoved the bullet into my sash and laughed. "Come on," I said. "You're going to love this."

We hiked down into a canyon, past yucca and sotol, until Gwen had to rest on a natural bench of rock, smoothed by wind, rain, and time. A dry wind blew and I offered Gwen some water from my canteen.

"I feel like such a weakling out here," she said.

"Air's thinner than what you're used to," I explained, "and this is a desert. If you get thirsty, drink. Besides, you're ten times better than those Washington scientists I brought out here."

"It is pretty," she observed.

I laughed. "Just wait."

We followed a dry creek bed deeper into the canyon, leaving the true desert behind and discovering an oasis where oaks merged with checker-barked juniper and agave. Mule deer grazed by another Mescalero roasting pit. The canyon was completely silent, except for the relaxing sound of running water.

When we reached the small stream, Gwen looked up and gasped. She had been looking at the ground while we walked, partly because she was tired and partly so she wouldn't trip or step on a snake. Now she saw the canyon walls and realized we were out of the desert.

Here maples and oaks, and higher up even aspen, exploded into a patchwork quilt of fall colors. Orange, red, yellow, and brown mixed with the evergreens and gold, white, gray, and slate of the canyon walls. Here the wind smelled of timber, and sunlight filtered through the leaves. Gwen breathed in the beauty of the place and knelt by the creek and splashed cold water on her neck and forehead.

"Colter, have you ever seen anything so beautiful?"

I was staring at her. "No," I responded, and there was a catch in my throat.

She looked at me and smiled. "New England has glorious falls, but this seems so much better, so primitive yet lovely, a garden of Eden. Thank you for sharing it with me."

I motioned up the trail. "There's a pretty good spot to eat about a mile more, if you feel up to it."

Gwen nodded at first, but then glanced at the water. "Colter?"

"Ma'am?"

"What I'd really like is a bath."

I stuttered and gurgled, trying to find some words, and Gwen laughed. Finally I suggested a deeper pool in the creek about a hundred yards away.

"I have your word that you won't spy on me?" she asked. "As a Texan and a gentleman?"

Now I've been called a lot of things before, but "gentleman" never was one of them. But I was a Texican, and deep down I reckon I was a gentleman.

I nodded and led Gwen to the spot. It wasn't really deep, but I guessed it would do. I gave Gwen my bandanna to use as a washrag, then climbed up the embankment and found a pleasant spot underneath a massive oak tree.

"This feels great!" Gwen shouted. "But it's cold!"

I twiddled my thumbs for a while, checked the revolver, finally pulled my hat down, and tried to take a nap.

A lot of folks have said that I spied on Gwen, but I swear I did no such thing.

Gwen called out that she was decent, and I turned around and offered my hand to help her up the embankment. I took her hand and pulled, but my moccasins slipped on the wet rocks and we both splashed into the creek. I cursed and groaned, but Gwen laughed furiously, and after jamming my soaking hat on my head, I chuckled some too, then helped her up.

She slipped again, but this time fell against me. I held her and she lifted her head and we stared at each other for a few seconds, silent. Romantics will tell you that there is a moment when you should kiss, but if you wait too long, the moment has passed.

The moment passed. Gwen blinked and started to back away. I never held much with romantics, so I pulled Gwen closer. She closed her eyes and we kissed.

"Well," she said when our lips parted.

I didn't know exactly how to respond, so I stuttered and gurgled some more. Gwen laughed and kissed me again.

* * *

We had our picnic, then made our way back to our horses. It was approaching dusk when we returned to the Pinery. The aroma of coffee and wood smoke was strong as I unsaddled our mounts and put them in the corral. Gwen kept me company while I finished my chore, then I took her hand and, smiling, we headed toward the camp.

Mr. McCarthy and Crutchfield sat by the fire, neither one of them looking up. "How was the hunting?" I asked, but they didn't respond. Jeff just shuffled his feet and played with his thumbs. Must have been bad, I thought and frowned. That meant rattlesnake for supper.

When I got closer I stopped suddenly. Jeff looked up frowning, and my eyes darted to the station and my right hand grabbed the butt of my revolver. Jeff's hands and feet were bound with rawhide. So were McCarthy's. Crutchfield had been trying to signal me, but I hadn't noticed. I had walked right into a trap.

Then I heard the voice, immediately recognizing the French accent that turned my stomach: "Colter! *Mon ami! Ciel,* but it is good to see you again!"

Alain Ruisseau stepped out of the station door, his massive LeMat revolver leveled at me.

Chapter Twenty

My hand moved away from the Starr revolver and dropped by my side. Ruisseau grinned, pulled on his overly waxed mustache with his left hand, and took a few more paces toward me. His revolver barrel remained leveled at me.

A LeMat is basically a hand-held cannon, a nine-shot revolver with an eighteen-gauge shotgun barrel, loaded with grapeshot, under the .40-caliber revolver barrel. Ruisseau could kill Gwen and me with one shot—and I knew he had no qualms about murdering a woman.

He was a swarthy man with black hair, wearing a fancy white shirt and open-sided, embroidered trousers of the French Dragoons. His hat was U.S. Army issue, and I figured he had killed the original owner. Ruisseau fought with Emperor Maximilian in Mexico until the patriots under Benito Juárez started winning, then he deserted, turning to the more profitable business of robbery and murder. The *Juáristas* had executed Maximilian and wanted to do the same to Ruisseau. There was a five-thousand-peso bounty on his head in Mexico, and another five-hundred-dollar reward for his capture in Texas.

A burly man with a bald head stepped out of the station, brandishing a Spencer rifle, and a bear-size, bearded Mexican with salt-and-pepper hair rounded the corner of the building, his right hand gripping the hilt of a machete. I recognized the Mexican from the Wanted posters plastered on walls from San Antonio to Tucson. Buitre Espina had killed at least twenty men, six with his bare hands, one for eighty-seven cents.

Bald Head barked something in German, and I assumed this was Otto, Ruisseau's right-hand man. Three other men emerged from their hiding places in the rocks and walked toward the campfire. So there were six of them, I thought, then heard footfalls behind me. No, seven.

Suddenly I caught the fragrance of jasmine perfume. A short, auburn-haired woman with dark eyes pulled the revolver and knife from my sash and tossed them toward Ruisseau. Our eyes met and she smiled.

''Hello, Rosebud,'' Waxahachie Kate said, then glanced at Gwen. ''Who's the hurdy?''

Just so there's no confusion, this was the original Waxahachie Kate—not her daughter, who took her ma's name and runs The Texas Palace in Dodge City. I met the original Kate when she was dealing faro in the red-light district of San Antone, had even cut the rug with her a time or two. She was a five-foot-one ball of fire, easy to like and a lot of fun—until she knifed some drummer who caught her cheating at poker. For more than two years, she had been on the owlhoot trail, watching the reward for her grow to fifty dollars and becoming the subject of a half-dime novel. Kate wore a pleated waist blouse and riding skirt and smelled great, but if she was riding with Ruisseau, she was as hardened as any man in the bunch.

She laughed, stood on her tiptoes, and gave me a peck on the lips. "Good to see you again, Rosebud. Alain will probably kill you, but it's good to see you." Then she joined her saddle pals.

Ruisseau finally holstered his LeMat and laughed again. He snapped his fingers and barked something in Spanish. The Mexican giant grabbed Mr. McCarthy and Crutchfield by their collars and effortlessly dragged them away from the fire and slammed them against the building. The Frenchman took their place by the fire and warmed his fingers, but his eyes never strayed off me.

"We see the tracks in the desert," Ruisseau explained. "The wagon is heavy, no? So I think perhaps they have finally found gold in these mountains, but, alas, we were fooled. Only a photographer's wagon. Perhaps *la mademoiselle* will take a daguerreotype of me, no?" He slapped his forehead. "Pardon, I have forgotten my manners."

Ruisseau stood, doffed his hat, bowed, and introduced himself. Gwen said nothing. I did the same, but Ruisseau just smiled. He snapped his fingers and ordered, "DeWitt, tobacco, *por favor.*" His Spanish was mocking.

One of Ruisseau's gunmen moved. He was a dark, unshaven man, and stood the closest to Gwen and me. He pulled one of several cigars from his shirt pocket and tossed it to Ruisseau, who took a stem from the fire and lit it. Satisfied, Ruisseau stared at Gwen. I didn't like the way he was looking at her. A moment later he spoke again, his cheery voice pricking my nerves. "*Mademoiselle,* do not be afraid. This man Colter and I are friends. Colter, is this not true?"

My mind was thinking. It was growing dark and Ruisseau liked to talk. Eventually, he would kill us, but if I could distract them, perhaps I could get Gwen to safety, hide her in the night, then come back and rescue her father and Jeff. Except for DeWitt, who stood in front of Gwen and me, they had gathered by the fire, about fifteen yards away.

Otto, the bald German, kept his Spencer cradled in his arms, and another man's right hand never let go of the revolver in his holster. I needed more time.

"I don't think friends is the right word," I finally said.

Ruisseau frowned. "*Oui,*" he said. "It would be hard to be friends with a man who killed your brother." He crossed himself, but Alain Ruisseau had no more feelings for his brother than he did for a rattlesnake. And he definitely wasn't religious.

Three years earlier, André Ruisseau tried to rob Rodolpho's place. I was there, drinking coffee, and when he saw me he panicked and started shooting. He fired three times but only managed to hit my tin cup.

I shot once, and Ruisseau dropped dead with a bullet in his heart. Killing a man is something I never took pride in, but I didn't grieve over André Ruisseau. He was a snake, a killer, a vile man who eventually would have hanged. My only regret was that it had been André, and not his older brother.

"But we should bury such things, Colter," Ruisseau said, and I knew he meant bury me. "But I had hoped to find a little more profit in this meeting. A camera is fine, but a lot of trouble. And your horse and *Monsieur* Crutchfield's are excellent animals, but, *ciel,* mules?"

I thought fast and slowly walked toward the man called DeWitt. Otto lifted his rifle, and even Kate drew the small but deadly Elliot's Pocket Revolver she carried in a shoulder holster. Slowly I pulled a cigar from DeWitt's pocket, bit off an end, and continued to the fire.

The outlaws relaxed when I squatted in front of them. Ruisseau continued as I found a stick to light the cigar. "Alas, *mon ami,* all we found was some gold and a few greenbacks in the wagon. Are you sure this is all the money you carry?"

My eyes quickly glanced at the canvas bag hanging from the station and back at Ruisseau. The Frenchman smiled and shook his head. "Colter," he said, "I am surprised at you. I do not miss much." I swore and tossed the stick into the fire—along with the .56-caliber cartridge Gwen had found that morning.

"Jernigan, see what's in that haversack," Ruisseau ordered as I walked toward Gwen.

A blond man in buckskin pants and a bib-front shirt hurried to the building, grabbed the sack, and shook it. The snake Crutchfield had killed dropped at his feet and Jernigan belched out curses and stumbled backward, never realizing the rattler was dead. About that time, the Spencer shell exploded in the fire, showering Ruisseau and his companions with sparks, smoke, and burning wood.

I dropped the outlaw named DeWitt with a roundhouse right to the jaw, grabbed Gwen's hand, and took off running, rounding the corner of the Pinery Station as a bullet whined and ricocheted off the wall.

Chapter Twenty-one

We rounded the next corner and I stopped suddenly, jerked Gwen beside me, and picked up the hoe leaning against the wall. When the man named Jernigan appeared, I let him have it. Gwen once killed a snake with the tool—and I broke a killer's nose and knocked him out cold. Dropping to my knees, I grabbed Jernigan's gun and fired just as the outlaw DeWitt rounded the corner.

The revolver was a London-made .38-caliber pepperbox, a rotating brass contraption that often misfired, which is what happened when I pulled the trigger. Instead of discharging one bullet, the pepperbox fired all six and sent the shiny revolver flying apart.

DeWitt was hurled back a good fifteen feet, dead before he hit the ground. On the other side of the station came Ruisseau's shouts and Otto's guttural grunts. Horses snorted and screamed, and the man named Jernigan groaned, slowly coming to. The outlaws had no idea that the pepperbox misfired and thus they were cautious, thinking I was now armed. I had bought us some time—but not much.

I tried to shake the pain out of my right hand. A

misfired pepperbox often did more harm to the shooter than the target, but I had been lucky. Quickly I turned to Gwen and whispered, ''I'm going to lift you onto the roof. Lie flat, keep quiet, and stay there—no matter what.''

With a boost, I helped her to the top of the station. In the growing darkness, Ruisseau might not notice her there. I doubted if he would expect me to leave her right under his nose, and she was probably safer here than she would be running with me through the desert.

I sprinted away from the station, hurdled a boulder, and took shelter behind a tree, waiting. Otto jumped from the far corner of the building and cut loose with a round from his Spencer, cursing when he realized I was gone. Ruisseau and the others appeared, and Kate kicked the stunned Jernigan and laughed.

Ruisseau's good humor had vanished, however, and he barked orders and told Kate to shut up. Holding my breath, I stared at the station roof. Gwen lay still— only inches above them. I rattled the limbs of the tree with a stick.

''There!'' a lean man in a black bowler shouted and sent a Winchester bullet in my direction. Squatting low, I took off running away from the station and toward the old stagecoach road.

Bullets whined through the night air, but darkness dropped on these mountains like a shroud and the outlaws were firing blind. All they needed was one lucky shot. I tripped once and swore, quickly regained my feet, and sprinted another forty yards before diving into an arroyo near the road. Flat on my back, I caught my breath. I could hear their shouts behind me.

"Henri!" Ruisseau yelled. "Fetch some lanterns! Jernigan! Watch Crutchfield and that old coot! Otto! Espina! Do you see them?"

Waxahachie Kate laughed. The German and the Mexican grunted and swore.

A half-mile up the road was a dark-walled canyon that dropped seventy or eighty feet to a fast-flowing stream. If I could make it there, I could climb down the canyon and hide. They would never find me in those shadows, and I could easily double back to the station. While they were searching for me, I could take care of Jernigan and hide the McCarthys. After that, Jeff Crutchfield and I would pay back Alain Ruisseau with interest.

The problem was getting to the canyon. I'd have to run in the open along the road. It grew darker by the minute, but it remained risky. Voices grew nearer, however, so I rolled out of the arroyo, took a deep breath, and sprinted up the road.

Again I tripped, tumbling off the road and landing with a thud on flat, cold granite. I gasped for air and listened. It was running water. I crawled fifteen feet and peered over the edge, staring into blackness. It was the canyon! I had almost run right past it. Suddenly I realized a new danger. This was darker than I expected. One wrong step and I could easily fall to my death. I began thinking of other options, when the orange glow of a lantern grabbed my attention. Someone was walking up the road, waving the lantern like a conductor signaling a train.

Now I had no choice. I lowered myself over the edge, groping for holds, unable to see anything. Light flowed above as I disappeared. I held my breath and pressed my body against the canyon wall. Spurs jingled and the lantern light cast eerie shadows that danced along the far side of the canyon. I looked up—directly into the bright lantern. The light blinded me temporarily and I closed my eyes.

Someone was holding a lantern just above me, but he hadn't spotted me—yet.

''See anything?'' someone asked.

''No. But I'm sure I heard something.'' It was Buitre Espina, and I could smell his foul breath.

The light dimmed slightly. Before I could relax, something clamped on my right hand and I was jerked up and thrown onto granite. The lantern sat at the edge of the surface, and the giant Mexican towered over me. He laughed and cracked his knuckles.

''Here!'' a voice cried behind me. ''Alain! Otto! We've found him!''

I had to move quickly—before the others arrived—so I jumped up and buried my fist in Espina's stomach. The brute didn't even grunt. Smiling, he sent a solid right to my temple. I felt as if he had buried an Apache war club in my brain.

The man behind me laughed. ''Mister, you shouldn't have done that. Buitre will tear you apart.''

I scrambled to my feet and charged Espina. He blocked my punches easily and again dropped me with one blow. I was slow to rise now. My vision was blurred. My ears were ringing. I wobbled and Espina grabbed me, lifted me over his head, and slammed me to the ground.

Breath whooshed from my lungs. When I could breathe again, Espina was bending over me, his sinister face glowing.

"Buitre, save him for me!" It was Alain Ruisseau's voice.

The Mexican rose, kicked my legs, and backed away. "Get up!" he commanded.

My right hand touched the side of the lantern and I yelped at the burn. The outlaws laughed, but their guffaws died when I grabbed the lantern and smashed it at Espina's feet. Coal oil splashed his boots and fire exploded. The giant shrieked and tumbled away from the blaze, beating out his burning clothes with his bare hands.

I fought for breath and tried to stand, but before I could recover a boot connected with my stomach and sent me sliding to the precipice. Coal oil burned along the rocks, so I could still see, though not clearly. Once again, Buitre Espina loomed over me. Hatred filled his dark eyes. He would burn eventually—of that Satan and I were certain—but my efforts at speeding up the process had failed.

"Buitre!" Ruisseau shouted. "He's mine!"

"No!" Espina replied angrily. "I kill him. Now."

I jumped to my feet and sent a fury of blows to Espina's face. He made no effort to block my punches and I hammered away, cutting his lips and busting his nose. Finally a giant hand grabbed my throat and Espina's death grip tightened.

He lifted me off my feet. My right hand grabbed his shirtfront, but Espina just smiled. Then my left hand found his machete and I tried to unsheathe it. This caught the killer by surprise and he backed away and dropped me. I sucked in air and jumped back just as Espina's machete clanged against the granite. The force of his delivery threw the Mexican off balance, and I kicked the man hard in the face. He dropped his weapon and reeled. Two rights staggered him back some more.

Finally I had momentum and continued to drive him, but within seconds I had to stop for breath. My chest heaved. Ruisseau shouted something, but I couldn't understand him. Espina ran his fingers through his beard, which absorbed most of the blood, and wiped his face.

"*Amigo,* you die now," he said, and laughed.

Well, two can play that hand, I thought and laughed with him. The Mexican looked at me dumbfounded and I reached forward and shoved him with both hands.

He lost his balance on the edge of the canyon and began flailing his arms. I kicked him in the knee and turned to run, but Espina's right hand latched onto my left arm like a vise. The killer shouted something in Spanish and fell over the edge, pulling me over with him as our screams melded together and we disappeared into complete darkness.

Chapter Twenty-two

*C*old. I was shivering. Hearing the babbling of water over rocks and songs of morning birds, I slowly opened my eyes. When I tried to move, sharp pain shot through the length of my body and I stilled myself for several minutes.

Just stay here and die, I thought, but gradually recalled Alain Ruisseau, Buitre Espina, and Gwen McCarthy. The image of Gwen got me moving again, though slowly. My legs were in the mountain stream but my upper body was on the rocky bank. I must have dragged myself to the shore before passing out after falling off the cliff with Espina.

My left arm hung awkwardly and I realized my shoulder had been pulled from its socket. Two fingers on my left hand were broken, several cracked ribs ached, and blood had crusted on my forehead over my left eye. I sucked in air, ignoring the burning pain in my chest, then I pulled the rest of my body out of the stream, rolled over, and fought back tears, pain, and nausea.

When I opened my eyes, I saw him.

Buitre Espina lay faceup in the middle of the rocky

stream, water flowing around his massive, motionless body. I knew immediately that he was dead. And I should have been. Later I guessed that his fat body had broken my fall, or maybe I landed in deeper water, or perhaps it was a combination of the two. All that really mattered was that I was alive. But I wouldn't stay alive if I didn't move quickly.

I slammed my shoulder back into place, and, yes, it was as painful as you imagine. My legs were numb, and walking was impossible. I had to get out of these wet clothes and dry myself by a fire, but how was I to get a fire going without my flint and steel? Staring at Espina's body, I noticed the yellow string hanging from his shirt pocket. I dragged myself through the stream to the dead bandit and pulled out the sack of cigarette tobacco, then rifled through the pocket. *There!* A small box of lucifer matches. And they were still dry! Unfortunately, Espina carried no weapon, but I had all that I needed for now.

After making my way to the bank, I crawled to a shallow cutback in the rocks, built a fire, and peeled off my clothes. The natural cavern would help block any smoke and reflect the fire's warmth. I massaged my legs until the blood was circulating again, made crude splints for my broken fingers, and fell asleep again.

When I woke up this time, my clothes were dry and I was hungry. That's a good sign, but I'd have to wait. I stumbled to my feet and walked around until I was sure I wouldn't fall, then picked up a good-size rock—

my only weapon—and made my way along the stream, circling back toward the Pinery Station.

For an hour, I studied our camp from a distance until I was certain Ruisseau and his gang had ridden away. I wasn't about to walk into another trap. With the exception of DeWitt's dead body, everything was gone: horses, mules, wagon—and Gwen no longer remained hidden on the roof. Ruisseau might have left someone behind just to make sure I was dead. Slowly I eased my way to the station and called out, ''Gwen?''

No answer. I had expected as much.

At first I guessed that Ruisseau had discovered Gwen and taken her with him, but tracks revealed that the outlaws had gathered everything—including Crutchfield and McCarthy—and headed down Guadalupe Pass, toward the Salt Flats and Franklin. Gwen had then climbed off the roof and followed them on foot. I gave up on trying to figure out why she would do a fool thing like that. She thought I was dead too. Instead of staying at the station, where someone would eventually happen by—although it might be Apaches or other outlaws—she took off after her father.

Why had Ruisseau taken Crutchfield and McCarthy with him? Maybe he thought Gwen would follow him and he could capture her, using her father as bait. Or maybe he just planned on dumping the two men in the Salt Flats and leaving them for buzzards. Whatever the reason, now I had to ask myself a question. Do I stay here, where I can survive, or go after them—on foot, without a weapon, into the desert? I already knew the answer, so I found a canteen gourd, filled it from the water barrel, and took a sip.

I spit the bitter liquid out and cursed loudly. Ruisseau was taking no chances with me, but it took one low coyote to poison water in a desert. After turning over the barrel to empty its lethal contents, I filled my gourd at the stream, then examined the building for anything I might need. Ruisseau's gang had picked the place clean. I checked DeWitt's body but found only some shot-to-pieces cigars and a dull pocketknife. I was hungry, though, and needed to eat before walking down the pass.

Looking at the ground, I frowned. There it was, unmoving, right beside the white haversack. With a groan I picked up the dead rattlesnake and began cleaning it with the dead outlaw's knife.

Dark clouds were gathering to the northwest when I reached the flats late that afternoon. Small footprints left by Gwen led straight into the unyielding expanse of stark white sand and finally disappeared.

A scientist once explained to me that the Salt Flats had been formed by what he called intermittent lakes. He went on to say that once this entire desert was covered by an ocean, though I found that hard to believe. Occasionally you could find a playa lake in this country, but usually any water here was too salty to drink.

With little vegetation except for a few yucca plants

and small desert shrubs, the flats drifted on for miles before reaching the Cornudas Mountains. After the lifeless Cornudas came the Hueco Mountains, and beyond that Franklin and Mexico. The nearest water would be at Ojos de los Alamos just over the New Mexican border, although it was possible to travel a straight line to the oasis at Hueco Tanks. Either way, it was a long, hot walk.

I wasn't worried. I had water and knew this country well. Gwen's tracks were easy to follow in the salt deposits; I could catch up with her, and by conserving our water we could survive. The wind was picking up and at the base of the Guadalupes, dark dust was rising almost as high as El Capitán. There was a big blow on its way, and that gave me cause for concern, so I hurried after Gwen.

The wind was already howling by the time I caught up with her, hiding behind a small yucca plant. It was dusk, but the clouds and approaching dust storm made it even darker. Gwen had taken a canteen with her into the desert, but she had already consumed half the water and was exhausted, slightly sunstroke, and delirious.

Seeing me didn't help matters. She thought I was a ghost, screamed, and tried to run, but I grabbed her shoulders and shook her.

"I'm alive! I'm alive! Everything will be all right!" I kept repeating until she finally comprehended that I wasn't a mirage and she bawled on my shoulder. I glanced back at the storm and helped her to her feet.

"We have to keep moving," I said, "with the wind." That yucca plant wouldn't provide enough shelter, and the blowing salt could tear the skin off a person. I ripped off a piece of her skirt and wrapped it around her face, then pulled my bandanna over my nose and hooked her arm as if we were going for a Sunday stroll.

"Keep your head down and your hands in your pockets!" I ordered. "Let's move!"

So we walked and stumbled with the wind, into the darkness as the temperature dropped, moving like cattle drifting in a blizzard, away from the old stagecoach road as sand and salt bit through our clothing. Finally we took shelter behind a small fort of yucca, wrapped ourselves together, and waited out the rest of the storm.

Chapter Twenty-three

At dawn we stared into the clear desert, now motionless and strikingly beautiful. Gwen smiled through chapped lips and said dryly, "I thought I was dreaming. It is you."

I returned the smile, though I didn't like everything I saw. Gwen had lost her canteen sometime during the windstorm, and the wind had forced us away from the road. I wasn't lost, but things could have been better.

"That Frenchman said you were dead," Gwen said and coughed. I gave her a sip of water. She wanted more but I pulled the gourd from her.

"Not too much," I said.

"He hates you," she said.

"Ruisseau? I know. He wouldn't get my vote for governor either." I told her about Ruisseau, about me killing his brother and what had happened at the cliff when Espina pulled me over. "This man," I said, tapping my chest lightly, "isn't so easy to kill. Ruisseau thinks I'm dead, though, and that'll give us an advantage."

I helped her to her feet and bit my lip. My ribs hurt, either from my long-winded speech or from lifting

Gwen. The gunshot wound in my arm throbbed again, and my broken fingers stung. I might be hard to kill, I said to myself, but I'm definitely mortal.

"We need to put some miles behind us before it gets too hot," I told Gwen. "We'll head back toward the road. Maybe someone will come by."

Her thoughts were miles away as she stared into the distance.

"We'll find them," I added softly. "We'll get your father and Jeff back . . . alive."

We stumbled along for miles without talking, conserving our strength. At noon we rested and Gwen ate the last of the rattlesnake meat I had saved. At the road, I discovered part of a rusty rim from a wagon wheel and used it to chop open a small cactus. The pulp was moist and tasteless, but it revived us a little, and we continued on until finding some shade.

This was November, but you couldn't tell. An unseasonal warm front had moved in, and the sun reflected off the fine sand, turning the Salt Flats into an oven.

"We'll rest here," I said, "until dark, then travel by night."

Walking by night was relatively safe here in the flats. We could avoid the sun and take advantage of the cool nights. Once we hit the rugged Cornudas, however, we'd be forced to travel during the day. At night in those mountains, a wrong step could break a leg or ankle, meaning a slow, certain death.

Gwen walked without complaint during the night

and we staggered along well past dawn before stopping for a sip of water and a breakfast of cactus.

"You all right?" I asked.

She nodded, unable to speak. So I helped her up again and we moved west. Although we walked along the stagecoach road there was no sign of anyone. By now my hopes for an Army patrol or any other miracle had evaporated. Despite the glaring sun, I wanted to travel at least another mile before waiting for nightfall. Gwen stopped suddenly and pointed ahead.

Heat waves rippled over the salt floor and I had to blink sweat from my eyes until my vision focused. I tried to swallow but couldn't. It was a body, about three hundred yards away, tied and left hanging between two tall yucca plants.

Gwen uttered something I couldn't understand, a wail or a groan, and took off running toward the body. I tried to tell her to save her energy but knew it was fruitless, so I followed her slowly, my hatred of Alain Ruisseau growing with every bitter step.

Jeff Crutchfield had been stripped to his long johns and tied to the cactus, spread-eagled, his head bent forward. They had left him to die, Apache-style, and Gwen was on her knees in front of him sobbing when I reached them.

I swore underneath my breath and fetched my knife, vowing that Ruisseau would pay for this. The dull blade bit into the ropes binding my partner's body and I sawed away, regretting that I wouldn't have the energy to waste on burying him. Finally, the last rope snapped and Crutchfield dropped to the salt floor with a thud.

Then he moaned.

I rolled him over gently. His face was badly sunburned, lips and tongue swollen. Gwen cradled his head and I opened the canteen and gave him a generous sip. He coughed and reached for the gourd but I pulled it away.

"Not now, partner," I said. Too much water would make him sick, maybe even kill him.

Slowly his eyes opened and he stared at me. "Colter?" he said, his voice barely audible. "You're alive," he stated.

"So are you." I tried to smile.

We found the nearest thing to shade and rested. I fed Jeff some cactus and even a lizard I managed to kill, figuring that a man who loved rattlesnake meat wouldn't mind another reptile. We stayed there all night, for Jeff was in no condition to walk. I gave him another sip of water at dawn.

His voice was raspy as he thanked me. "They're keepin' McCarthy drunk," he said. "It amuses Alain." He coughed violently and groaned.

"Don't talk, Jeff," I said. "I'll ask questions. You blink. Once for yes, twice for no. Understand."

"Yes," he said.

"Blink! Don't talk. Blink."

His eyes blinked once.

"You know where they're headed?"

One blink.

"Ojos de los Alamos?"

Two blinks.

"Hueco Tanks?"

One blink.

"Still five of them?"

One blink.

"Did Ruisseau mention Culbertson?"

Another yes answer.

"Think he'll keep the old man alive as far as the tanks?"

Crutchfield shrugged, then blinked once.

"Can you walk?"

A heavy sigh followed two blinks.

"Get some rest," I said and stood up. Gwen stared at me and I motioned for her to follow as I walked toward a dead yucca twenty feet from Crutchfield.

"Your father's alive," I said, but she already knew this. "I don't think Ruisseau will kill him, not for a while. Ruisseau's heading to Hueco Tanks. What he doesn't know is that there's an Army patrol stationed there now. With luck, those soldiers will kill Ruisseau and send a patrol out after us once your father tells them what happened."

She forced a smile, but I could tell she didn't believe me. It was a long shot, but at least a chance. Ruisseau might spot the Army first, but he had a camera wagon and stolen stock he would want to sell before heading into Franklin and back into Mexico. J. D. Culbertson would have to meet him, probably at the tanks, to cut a deal.

Culbertson owned a ranch just east of Franklin, but he was rumored to deal in rustled livestock and stolen merchandise. Some said he was a Comanchero, trading powder and guns, merchandise—even women—with the Comanches. No one had ever proved this, however, so Culbertson roamed free.

Ruisseau would have to wait for Culbertson and then they'd haggle over a price for the horses, guns, and "What-Is-It Wagon." That would give us some time, and if Alain was having fun keeping Stephen McCarthy drunk, I figured he'd keep the old man alive—at least until he and Culbertson reached a deal. Ruisseau might even sell McCarthy to Culbertson, who in turn could trade the old man to the Comanches as a slave. The Indians liked their captives younger and stronger, but McCarthy would be worth something.

That explained why Ruisseau was keeping the old man alive and drunk.

Of course, I'd never catch up to Ruisseau in time. Alone, I might stand a chance, but I couldn't leave Gwen and Jeff. And now I'd have to carry Jeff myself. The Army would have to take care of Alain Ruisseau, and Stephen McCarthy would need God's help.

I lifted Jeff and stumbled ahead of Gwen toward the faint outline of the Cornudas Mountains. My moves were mechanical after a while. The sun baked through my hat and fried my brain. Often we had to rest, losing count of the times we tripped or stumbled.

When I became too exhausted to carry Jeff by myself, Gwen helped. We each draped an arm over our shoulders and half-carried, half-dragged him toward the mountains, stopping to feed ourselves on the last of the cactus and small sips from our dwindling supply of water.

Early the next day while carrying Jeff by myself I stumbled and fell. The side of my right hip struck a sharp rock and I felt something running down my buckskin pants. At first I thought I was bleeding but upon sitting up, I realized it was something far worse. Our canteen gourd had been smashed by the rock.

Our water was gone.

Chapter Twenty-four

Sucking on pebbles helped lessen our thirst, but not much. By the following day, the mountain range looked no closer and heat waves still rippled across the white sand. Barely able to talk and no longer sweating, I was mostly dragging Jeff by now.

Gwen fell to her knees, groaning, and I waited for her to rise. I didn't dare ease Jeff to the ground because I wasn't sure I'd be able to lift him again. Slowly Gwen struggled to her knees, wiped sand off her face, and stared beyond me.

She was up and running toward a blue spot maybe two hundred yards away. I tried to call for her to stop, but through parched lips and a swollen tongue only managed to hack. Studying the blue speck, I soon realized it wasn't a mirage. There was no choice, so I dropped the unconscious Crutchfield and weaved awkwardly after Gwen.

I tackled her just as she reached the water hole. She screamed as I pulled her away, even slapped me. "Water!" she shouted, her voice barely recognizable. I kept her pinned until she quit struggling. Slowly I rose, glanced at the water and back at her.

"Let me check it first," I said hoarsely.

Gwen lay still as I crawled five yards to the shallow hole, cupped my hands, and tasted the water. As soon as my back was turned, she jumped up and dived toward the hole, but my right hand shot out and pulled her away, throwing her hard to the ground.

"It's water!" she wailed and sent a flung a handful of sand at me but her throw was weak, her aim poor.

I spit out the liquid. "Pure brine," I said. "Salt. Make you sick."

"Nooooo!"

She cried without tears as I dragged her away, back to Jeff where she finally fell asleep. Somewhere I had lost the dull pocketknife, so I smashed a cactus with the rusty rim I still carried and ate more cactus. It wasn't enough.

We'd never make it out of this furnace.

At dusk, Gwen woke up and ate her share of cactus. She apologized for her hysteria, but I shook my head.

"My fault," I said. "Should have taken you back to the Pinery." Actually, I was thinking that I never should have brought her out here to begin with. I should have left the McCarthys at Borachio Station.

Weakly she held out her hand and I clasped it. We said nothing for several minutes, just looked into each other's eyes. I thought about our picnic in the canyon, about the first time we kissed. We were going to die out here in a matter of days. But not yet. I told Gwen that I wasn't easy to kill, and I meant it.

"Let's move," I ordered.

I pulled her up and she rested her head against my chest. "I love you, Raleigh Colter," she said.

Lifting her chin, I stared at her, forgetting my earlier thoughts, no longer regretting my decision to guide her to the mountains. "We're getting out of here. Me, you, and Jeff." My voice cracked with pain but I continued. "Maybe we can find a preacher in Franklin and get hitched."

"That a proposal?"

"Not a very good one, but, yeah."

"I accept," she rasped.

It took every bit of strength I had to pull Jeff to his feet. He still couldn't walk on his own, remained barely conscious, so it was hard going, but I blocked everything out while I struggled on, sucking on pebbles, concentrating on those distant mountains.

I have no idea how long we walked—hours or days—or how many times I fell. My memories disappeared in the barren flats. It was midday when I stumbled again, only when I looked up the base of the Cornudas Mountains were clear, just fifty more yards. It looked shady over there. I tried to swallow but couldn't and rolled over.

Jeff and Gwen lay unconscious beside me. Standing up and walking became impossible, so I took a firm grip on Gwen's blouse and crawled toward the shade, dragging her behind me. A turtle could have moved faster. I would mark a rock in front of me and crawl toward it, vowing to rest when I reached the spot. Once there, however, I'd pick another rock and continue on without stopping. Finally I was there, at the Cornudas.

I placed Gwen against the brown rocks, out of the sun, and stared back at the Salt Flats. Slowly I crawled toward Jeff, reached him, and pulled him in the same fashion out of the brutal frying pan and to the cooler, but just as lifeless, mountain range.

It hurt to breathe. I saw a cactus and pulled myself to it, took my wagon wheel rim, and hacked away. Exhausted, I collapsed and looked at the cactus. My thoughts cleared and I realized the plant was brown, dried up, and dead.

Like us, I thought and rolled away.

"I'm sorry," I told Gwen, though she was asleep and too far away to have heard me anyway. At least she's in the shade. "I love you, Gwen McCarthy," I whispered, wanting to crawl back to her, so that we would die in each other's arms, but I was unable to move. Slowly I closed my eyes, trying to think of a prayer.

When I woke up, I stared into the black, malevolent eyes of Death.

Things were hazy, and even now I have no idea what actually happened and what I dreamed. I was vaguely aware of motion. At some point I felt as though I were actually flying—like a golden eagle. My dreams were mostly of Gwen, but Alain Ruisseau made some appearances.

At least twice I woke up screaming, then felt a soft

hand steady me and lean me back into a soft bed. I smelled coffee and tasted broth. When I opened my eyes, I saw my mother—dead these many years. She smiled and made me eat my soup, caressed my face, and changed the bandage on my arm, the splints holding my broken fingers.

She spoke softly and I finished my soup and went back to sleep, wondering why she was talking to me in Spanish.

We were loaded into the "What-Is-It Wagon," which transformed into a hearse, and bounced across the Salt Flats, through the mountains, and all the way to a church in Franklin. Gwen stepped out in a white wedding gown, followed by a band of Apaches. A silver-haired Mescalero took my hand, put me in a bed, and spooned soup into my mouth.

I was traveling again, pulled by a travois. Someone was singing, but it wasn't *Rock of Ages.* Dreams took over. I danced with Gwen in the canyon stream in the Guadalupes. A mountain lion purred and curled up at Gwen's feet like a house cat. We dined at The Drovers Cottage in Abilene, where I ordered—of all things—rattlesnake. I walked outside, mounted Dollie, and galloped to Fort Davis, where I easily won all of the soldiers' pay with my trick shooting. Everything I aimed at looked like Alain Ruisseau's face.

I never missed.

Groaning, I opened my eyes again. I stared at a ceiling of sticks, straw, and thatch and breathed in the pleasing aroma of venison, horses, and mescal. Slowly

I sat up. I was on a straw bed covered with a saddle blanket. A bowl of food was at my feet and a tin cup of coffee beside it. Both were cold, but I devoured food and drink, then lay back down.

This is not a dream, I said to myself, closing my eyes. I was in an Apache wickiup. At least, I thought I was. But how? And where were Gwen and Jeff? Immediately I heard movement, felt the wind and knew someone was beside me. I forced open my eyes. Death again stared back at me, his face painted black, dark hair hanging from under a heavily beaded buckskin war cap.

''Demonio,'' I said.

Chapter Twenty-five

A toothless, prune-faced Mescalero woman bent over Gwen, applying some sort of salve to her sun-burned face and cracked lips. Demonio had led me to this wickiup, where Jeff and Gwen slept peacefully. The Apache leader grunted something and the woman barked back angrily, shoving me and Demonio out of the lodge.

I guess the woman noticed the worry in my eyes because as soon as we were outside, she stopped her contortions and mumbled something softly. "She says your woman and friend will be fine," Demonio translated in Spanish. She looked at Demonio, then me, nodded once, and disappeared inside the hut.

"We will talk some more," Demonio said and walked away.

The Mescalero camp was in a canyon, well hidden, in what I took for the Hueco Mountains. Instead of being surrounded by tarbush, yucca, and other desert scrubs, the walls were lined with juniper and Arizona oaks. Two Apache maidens filled their gourds at a sizable water hole at the edge of the oasis.

I knew this area better than any man around, yet

this place was foreign to me. This wasn't Hueco Tanks, where rock basins trapped rainwater, nor was this Ojos de los Alamos or any other water hole I had seen.

Demonio read my mind. "White men have not learned of this place," he said. "It is known only to *Indeh.*"

"It is a good place," I said.

He nodded and motioned for me to sit on a boulder in front of him.

I wore a new deerskin shirt provided by the Apaches for my old shirt had been ripped to pieces while crossing the Salt Flats. My buckskin pants and Apache moccasins had fared well, and I still had my sash and hat, although both were grimy by now. I did not, however, carry any weapon. Even the rusty rim was gone.

"You have been with us two days," Demonio said.

I told him what had happened, how Alain Ruisseau had surprised us and taken the wagon and Gwen's father away, probably to deal with the Comancheros. Demonio's face never changed expression, although he did spit when I mentioned Comancheros. He didn't have much use for Comanches or white traders. Minutes passed before he spoke after I completed my tale.

"It is bad that the woman has lost her magic box," he finally said. "It is bad that her power is now in the hands of an enemy."

Awkward silence returned. I couldn't ask for help.

Demonio would consider that a sign of weakness. He couldn't offer help because, deep down, we were enemies and maybe he was a little concerned that Ruisseau had Gwen's so-called power. This was a fight between white men, not Apaches.

"We leave tonight," Demonio said. I had been so lost in thought that his voice startled me. "You cannot come with us, but we shall leave you where our grandfathers drew the paintings in the caves by the place that holds water." That was a lot of Spanish for me to run through my head and translate, but I understood that he meant Hueco Tanks. "This is all I can do."

"It is enough, Demonio," I said. "You have given us our lives."

"You might not keep them for long," he added as he rose. "The enemies you seek camp at that place."

I entered the wickiup and knelt beside Gwen, leaned over, and kissed her gently on the lips. Her eyes opened and she smiled. "Hey," she said, "I'm alive."

"We all are, thanks to Demonio."

Sitting beside her and stroking her hair, I told her what had happened. "The Apaches are breaking camp tonight," I concluded. "They're going to leave us at Hueco Tanks." I paused. "Ruisseau is still there."

"Father?"

I nodded. A Mescalero scout had watched the tanks and reported to Demonio that afternoon. Ruisseau's men arrived four days ago, noticing the America flag flapping in the wind at the old stagecoach station.

They snuck in at night, apparently killing the soldiers stationed there. A rider went out the next day, while the others stayed at camp, finishing their whiskey and making an old man fetch water, cook for them, and wash their clothes.

Yesterday morning, Ruisseau's rider returned with three men. There was a celebration that lasted well into the night. There was drinking and eating, but mostly drinking, until the moon was sinking and they were all asleep. The Apache brave thought about going down there while they were passed out and killing them all but had decided against it, recognizing the "What-Is-It Wagon" and remembering the power of the magic box.

So he had ridden back to Demonio's camp this morning, while the white men stumbled around the water tanks with their hangovers.

What this meant, I reasoned, what that J. D. Culbertson had joined Ruisseau, bringing two gunmen with him in case the Frenchman got greedy. That meant there would be eight of them. I'd have to hide Gwen and Jeff in the rocks—Crutchfield was too weak to fight—and knock them off one at a time.

"What are you going to do?" Gwen asked.

"I have a plan," I lied and stood up to leave.

"Colter?" she called out when I reached the wickiup's entrance. I turned.

"That proposal you made in the desert?" She smiled. "I won't hold you to it."

I walked back and knelt beside her again. "That 'I

accept' you said in the desert?'' I leaned over and kissed her. ''I'm holding you to it.''

True to his word, Demonio left us a mile from the tanks well past midnight. Clouds blocked out the moon and stars, and the wind whipped fiercely. A norther was blowing in, and it felt like it would turn into a wet one.

''You will fight your enemies alone?'' Demonio asked.

''I do not wish him to have the magic box,'' I replied.

The Apache leader turned to Gwen. ''This man you have,'' he said, ''is good. I wish he were *Indeh.*''

I tell you, that compliment made my head swell, and I wouldn't trade it for a medal from George Washington or handshake from Sam Houston. Demonio kicked his horse and rode away, followed by the other Mescaleros, disappearing into the dark night.

Lots of folks have since told me that I owed that Apache nothing. He didn't leave me any weapon, didn't offer to help, just dumped me in the desert unarmed and outnumbered eight to one. But I never saw it that way. He gave us our lives—at least twice— which took some doing considering that he had sworn to kill every white man in his land. When the Army raided his camp and killed him two years later at Manzanita Spring, I was probably the only white man to shed tears.

*   *   *

We eased our way just off the road toward the land-mark of rocks that shot up some three hundred feet from the desert. When I led the government expedition from the Guadalupes to Franklin and stopped here, one of the scientists called the rock "syenite porphyry." I liked Hueco Tanks better.

The place was an oasis in the rugged terrain be-tween the Cornudas Mountains and Franklin, sur-rounded by the Chihuahuan Desert. Most of the small, dark mountains were smooth, with caves carved by wind and rain. Oaks and junipers were abundant around the *huecos* that held water for animals and trav-elers.

Jeff and Gwen protested, but I left them in a small cave around dawn and crawled toward the ruins of the old stagecoach station. My hand touched cold flesh and I leaped back, but in the approaching dawn I made out the body's blue uniform and slowly saw three other corpses. It was the Army patrol stationed here, brutally murdered and dumped without a proper burial. I swore and moved on until I was at the side of the station.

Voices grumbled, wood cracked in a fire, and the smell of coffee and bacon made my stomach knot. "All right, Alain," someone said. "Let's look at that wagon again."

I massaged my hands to get the blood moving. The temperature had dropped forty degrees during the night and the wind made it that much colder. Slowly I rose, found a four-foot limb in the woodpile, and peered around the corner of the crumbling adobe wall.

A man in a bowler hat warmed himself by the fire. Stephen McCarthy was asleep, bound from head to toe and thrown against the station wall like a sack of flour. The outlaw coughed and read a newspaper to himself. I looked around. Everyone else was gone.

"Cures con-sump-tion, bron-chi-tis, and all lung dis-eases," he slowly read out loud from an advertisement. It was one of Ruisseau's men, Henri, I think, a pale, bony cuss with my Starr revolver stuck in his holster.

He heard me grunt and turned, dropping the *Harper's Weekly* and reaching for his—my—revolver. I swung the limb like an ax, striking him hard across his head and sending him to the ground with a thud and the paper scattering in the wind.

I was on top of him in an instant, but he was knocked cold. Quickly I pulled the revolver from his holster, and then I caught the scent of jasmine perfume. I swore as I turned around; something flashed beneath my eyes and caught me hard below my nose. There was the taste of metal and blood in my mouth as I fell beside the fire.

When my head cleared seconds later, I was staring at Waxahachie Kate. Her six-barrel Elliot's Pocket Pistol was pointed at my heart and her finger was cradling the trigger.

"Hello, Rosebud," she said.

Chapter Twenty-six

Dressed up, Waxahachie Kate could be a dazzling woman, but this morning she donned greasy buckskins, her eyes were bloodshot and she wore too much rouge to hide what looked like a bruise on her left cheek. No doubt, she had mouthed off to Alain Ruisseau once too often. That tiny ten-dollar revolver pointed at me didn't make her any more attractive.

Slowly I sat up and my right hand inched toward the Starr revolver a couple of feet from me. Kate shook her head and her finger tightened on the trigger. I brought my hand back to my side, spit out blood, and ran my tongue over my teeth to make sure she hadn't knocked any out. I was lucky.

"That hurt," I said.

"I don't know how you survived falling off that cliff, Rosebud," she said, "but I think you've used up your ninth life. I should kill you now."

"Why would you want to kill me?" My hand began creeping toward the revolver again.

"One more inch and you're dead, Colter." My hand stopped. "Maybe I'd kill you so Alain won't stake you to an anthill. A bullet's faster, kinder. Maybe I'd kill you because it hurt me to see you taking a shine to that hurdy.''

Her voice was full of sarcasm—at least I think it was sarcasm—but I realized that she probably would kill me if I forced her hand. I looked at my Starr again and knew that, unlike Kate, I could never kill her. I was a dead man. It was just a question of when.

''Let me free the old man, Kate,'' I pleaded, motioning toward the still-sleeping Stephen McCarthy. ''A trade. Him for me. I give you my word that I won't try anything.''

''No deal, Rosebud. Alain's selling that old codger to Culbertson. Gonna make him a Comanche slave. I let him go and there goes my cut.

''Where is that gal of yours, Rosebud?'' Kate asked suddenly.

I shrugged. Kate gestured with her pistol. ''She's right behind you, Kate,'' I said.

She laughed, shaking her head, then heard something behind her. Her eyes widened and she spun around.

I had seen those Federal soldiers at Fort Stockton play baseball that summer, hitting a cowhide ball with a bat and running around bases on the parade ground. It was an interesting game—the first time I had seen it played. Being from the East, Gwen McCarthy must have been a big fan of the sport because she held that tree limb with both hands and swung it like a bat as Kate turned around.

The wood connected with a thud against Kate's

head and she dropped like a boulder beside me, the Elliot's Pocket Pistol clanging against the rocks. Gwen hovered over her, still wielding the tree limb like a weapon, her eyes blazing, and spat out, "Trollop!"

I shoved the Starr in my sash and bent over Kate. Actually, I thought Gwen had killed her, but Kate was still breathing. "Untie your father!" I ordered, grabbed a lariat hanging on the adobe wall, lifted the unconscious Waxahachie Kate, and carried her across the yard to a small cave in the mountainside. I laid her among the rocks, gagged her with her bandanna, and hog-tied her with the lariat.

Next I dashed back to the station and carried the man called Henri to the cave. He weighed less than Kate. Leaving him gagged and tied in the same fashion as Kate, I ran back and gathered a couple of bedrolls and used these to wipe out my trail to the cave. I also covered Kate and Henri with the blankets, partly, I reckon, to keep them warm but mostly to make them that harder to see.

Gwen and her father were waiting by the station when I returned, erasing my trail with the last blanket. I gave the dirty piece of wool to Mr. McCarthy, picked up Kate's pistol, and handed it to Gwen.

"Get back to Jeff," I said. "Circle around the near mountain about a quarter of a mile and climb. Halfway up you'll see a rock formation that looks like a broken eggshell. Hide there and stay there no matter what. It's going to get colder, so huddle close."

"But—" Gwen began.

"No buts! Move it!"

Gwen kissed me on the cheek and took off running, pulling her groggy father by the hand. I peered into the old station and saw the Winchester Yellow Boy leaning against the wall. Inside the room I checked the weapon, sighing with relief that it was loaded, and rifled through the place for anything else I might need. I picked up an old Confederate shell jacket off the floor, tying the long sleeves across my waist. The wool clothing might come in handy if it got really cold.

Then I stepped outside and froze.

The outlaw called Jernigan stood ten feet in front of me, and about a hundred yards behind him came Alain Ruisseau and the rest of the bandits.

Jernigan was rubbing his heavily bandaged nose and looking down as he walked toward the station, so when his head jerked up he was just as surprised as I was. His right hand shot down and tugged at a holstered revolver.

I fired from the hip with the Winchester, jacked another round into the chamber, and pulled the trigger again. The first shot spun Jernigan around and the second finished him. I was racing across the yard before he hit the ground, firing as I ran.

"Colter!" Ruisseau screamed.

There was no way I could hit them this way, but my scathing fire kept them dancing and diving for cover. The German Otto recovered first and sent two shots from his Spencer repeater in my direction. He was an excellent marksman. His first bullet burned my neck and the second splintered the stock of the Winchester.

My rifle was empty by now, so I tossed it aside and dived the remaining five yards behind the rocks along the base of the mountain. Two more bullets whined off boulders. Another clipped a juniper branch over my head.

I sucked in air and drew my Starr. Henri had loaded all six chambers, and for that I was glad. Usually I kept one chamber empty as a safety measure.

''Kill him!'' Ruisseau screamed. ''I want his head!''

''Kate! Henri!'' the German shouted.

''They're probably dead! Culbertson, there's five hundred dollars if you kill Colter! Another fifty if he's alive so that I can cut out his heart.''

''You heard him. Larry, Miguel. We'll flush him out.''

''You're a dead man, Colter!'' Ruisseau's final words echoed off the walls. Ice began bouncing off my hat and clothes. Sleet! The wind cut through me like a knife. I had six shots and there were five men after me.

I rolled over and climbed over the smooth but slick rocks and up the mountain, which became a maize through oaks, junipers, and strange rock formations. I guessed that the men chasing me would split up. That might improve my odds, but not greatly. I moved quickly, climbing higher, heading east toward the *huecos*. A half hour later, sleet covered the ground and twice my moccasins slipped and sent me sprawling against the sharp rocks.

Cold air burned my lungs, my broken fingers throbbed, and cracked ribs ached. Scrambling up the mountain, I suddenly found myself at a dead end with no way to go but down. I cursed myself and turned back but only made it ten yards before someone shouted.

J. D. Culbertson stood fifty yards up the trail. His face was hidden by a massive beard that matched the heavy buffalo coat he wore, and the brim of his black slouch hat flapped in the wind. He spit out a stream of tobacco juice, raised his Henry rifle, and sent a bullet humming past my right ear.

I dropped to my knees, quickly aimed, but managed to hold my fire. *Wait for a better shot!* Another bullet ricocheted off the rocks, so I inched my way back to the edge and peered below.

''I think I got him, boys!'' Culbertson shouted.

It wasn't as bad of a drop as I had originally thought. Shoving the Starr back in my sash, I grasped a juniper branch and lowered myself as far as I could go. Musical spurs warned me that Culbertson was running toward me, so I let go and dropped about twenty feet onto a rock ledge. My feet slipped on the ice and I fell hard against the stone, pain shooting through my chest and causing me to moan. I rolled over and slid off the ledge, falling another six feet into a bed of brambles and ferns.

About that time I heard J. D. Culbertson scream.

I opened my eyes to see that massive heap of brown falling hard, arms flailing. His boots must have slipped on the ice and sent him cascading down the mountainside, only he took the long way down, bouncing off boulders and tree branches and finally landing with a splash in one of the water tanks.

His Henry rifle clattered among the rocks on the ledge above me, out of my reach. I was going to try to climb up for it, but one of Culbertson's gunmen looked over the edge and saw me. I rolled out of the way just as a bullet smashed the place where my head had been. A cave opened before me and I lunged inside.

I was out of the sleet, but the cavern was small and narrow and there was only one way out. Within minutes, Culbertson's men had me trapped.

"Amigo," a voice called out. *"Vaya con Dios."*

A gunshot exploded and the bullet ricocheted over my head and bounced around the rock walls surrounding me, buzzing like an angry hornet.

Chapter Twenty-seven

The first bullet had barely stopped dancing when two more gunshots barked and slugs whined and popped back and forth against the hard, dark walls of my cave. Something stung me in the chest and I slapped my shirt, catching a piece of lead in my right hand. The bullet was spent when it hit me, but I knew my luck wouldn't hold out.

"Let me try, Miguel," someone drawled. The Mexican outlaw's reply was drowned out by the massive report of a heavy pistol. Instead of ricocheting, though, this bullet splintered against the far wall. One piece grazed my cheek.

"Too much gun, Larry," the Mexican said and fired twice more.

I hugged the ground and covered my head as the bullets screamed past me with terrifying whines. Something bit into my right thigh and I felt warm blood oozing down my leg.

My cave was turning into a coffin.

"*Amigo*, are you still alive?"

I sat up, pulled off my bandanna, and tied it over my leg. The bullet had cut through muscle and exited cleanly, missing the bone, but soon I would be shot to pieces.

"*Amigo?*"

"I'm still breathing!" I shouted back. There was no use in playing possum, hoping that they might enter the cave and step into the sights of my revolver. They'd keep shooting until they were sure I was dead.

"You should come out now. Else you gonna look like a piece of Swiss cheese." It was the American's voice. "What you say?"

If I stayed here, I was dead. Would they shoot me as soon as I stepped outside, or take me back to Ruisseau? Of course they'd lead me back to Ruisseau, so he could take pleasure in torturing me to death and they could collect the extra fifty dollars for bringing me back alive. I might have a chance to escape later. It was a gamble, but I had no choice.

"All right!" I yelled. My voice echoed in the narrow cavern. "I'm coming out. Hold your fire."

"*Amigo.* Pitch your revolver out first, *por favor.*"

I tossed the Starr into the daylight and stepped out of the cavern. Larry and Miguel grinned fiendishly with anticipation but kept their revolvers trained on me. Sleet bounced off my hat and my breath was frosty as I sized up my captors.

In spite of the cold, the Mexican wore wooden sandals, dark trousers, and a cowhide vest covering his flannel shirt. His hat was brown and plain, open crowned with a turkey feather stuck in the back. A rock amulet hung around his neck, and he cradled an

Army Colt in his right hand. He may have been a half-breed, but I was certain he was a Comanchero.

The American had black teeth and a bushy red mustache, and I had never been partial to redheads. His moth-eaten clothes and battered Confederate campaign hat were covered in dirt. I could smell him from where I stood. He carried a big New Orleans boot pistol, a .50-caliber single-shot weapon preferred by gamblers who wanted a little more substance than a derringer offered.

They hadn't killed me yet. That's a good sign, I said to myself.

"Hands on the rocks, friend," Larry said. "Miguel. Better search him."

With my hands held over my head, I turned around and leaned forward, gripping the rock wall with both hands and waited for the Mexican to search me. His rough hands bounced across my bloody thigh and cracked ribs, causing me to groan and him to laugh. Satisfied, he stepped back and said, "Let's go, *amigo*."

His use of the word *amigo* irritated me considerably.

I sighed, deciding that it was time to play my hand now rather than wait for something better. My right hand gripped a hefty rock and I turned around, favoring my wounded leg. Miguel stood just a few feet in front of me; Larry was ten yards farther back. My left hand dropped quickly to my side, and the Mexican's eyes followed its movement. With my right hand, I hurled the stone forward with all my might and lunged at Miguel.

The rock struck him in the forehead and caused him to drop his Colt. I reached him as he staggered back, grabbed his left arm, and pulled him in front of me as a shield, turning him around to face Larry and clamping my left forearm against his windpipe.

Larry's boot pistol boomed. The slug slammed into Miguel's chest and the impact sent us both reeling against the icy mountainside. My head bounced against the rocks as I slid down while the Mexican dropped dead beside me.

This wasn't exactly what I had planned.

I figured Larry would hold his fire, but the fool panicked. Now I was without a hostage, but Larry stood dumbfounded, staring at Miguel's lifeless body. His single-shot pistol was also empty.

"You done killed Miguel!" Larry shouted.

I didn't argue with him, though he had pulled the trigger. I found my feet, lowered my shoulder, and dived into him before he could regain his wits. We crashed into the brambles, and I sent several blows to his head and ripped the empty pistol out of his hand.

His left fist rocked into my head and I rolled off him, staggered to my knees, and slammed the pistol barrel against his temple as he tried to stand. Groaning, he fell beside his dead companion.

It took me several minutes to catch my breath. Thunder sounded in the distance as I tied and gagged Larry and rolled him into the cave, taking a couple of pieces of jerky from his shirt pocket. Next I checked the bullet wound in my thigh. It was clean, and the cold weather had slowed the bleeding, so I replaced my makeshift bandage and limped toward the *huecos.*

I had to check on Culbertson, to make sure he was dead. Sleet bounced off the massive hunk of buffalo fur in the shallow water of the nearest water tank. If the fall hadn't killed him, the exposure would, and J. D. Culbertson was quite dead now. His days of dealing with the Comanches and men like Alain Ruisseau were over. Gripping his heavy coat, I managed to pull his body from the water and leave him on the ground. I didn't want him to foul up drinking water in the desert.

Slowly I untied the shell jacket and pulled it over my deerskin shirt. Finding a hiding place in case Otto or Ruisseau came by, I ate the jerky and tried to think.

Kate, Henri, and Larry were out of it—providing that Ruisseau hadn't found my prisoners in the cave by the old Butterfield building and freed them. Miguel, Jernigan, and Culbertson were dead. That left only two, but those were Alain Ruisseau and Otto, the worst of the bunch.

The sleet finally died but thunder echoed again, only now I realized my mistake. It wasn't thunder. It was gunfire—and it was close.

''Gwen!'' I said out loud and took off toward the hiding place.

Halfway up the mountain I knew I had made another error. My Starr revolver was back in my sash, but I had left the other weapons by the water tanks. Culbertson's Henry rifle, even Miguel's Colt revolver, would come in handy. It wasn't too late to go back, but I was drawn toward the rock formation shaped like a broken eggshell. I had to make sure my companions were all right, then return for more artillery.

My wounded leg and treacherous ice made the going slow. My eyes darted, studying everything as I moved among the rocks and trees. Finally I slid my back against the cold wall of the mountain and cautiously peered around the corner at the hiding place.

A campfire blazed in the center of camp, about twenty yards in front of the concave rock. Alain Ruisseau sat in front of it, smiling, warming his hands. About twenty feet to his right were the McCarthys and Jeff Crutchfield, the latter bleeding from a gash across his forehead. Their hands and feet were bound with rawhide.

I cursed myself. I should have left Jeff and Gwen with something better than Waxahachie Kate's little pistol, which was only good at close range. Otto could have easily flushed them out with his long-range rifle, which is what I guessed had happened.

''Colter!'' Ruisseau cried out, his voice echoing. He couldn't see me, but he knew I was close. ''Come to me, Colter! Let us finish this like gentlemen!''

Gentlemen! Ruisseau made me sick.

Finally I saw Otto. The big German was in the trees about twenty yards away, sort of catercorner from Ruisseau, his rifle barrel pointed toward the

McCarthys and Jeff. I couldn't hit him from my position, so I'd have to get closer, and there was only one way to do that.

Slowly I pulled off the jacket and dropped it on the ground. It would hinder my movements and aim. I'd have to walk right into the camp and count on Ruisseau's mean streak, hoping he'd want to toy with me first before killing me.

''Colter!'' Ruisseau's cold cry ricocheted off the walls again. I tugged at the Starr revolver in my sash and walked toward the fire.

Chapter Twenty-eight

In the 1879 Beadle's Half-Dime Library novel *This Man Colter: Or, Harrowing Adventures of the Texas Borderman and His Belle*, the honorable Colonel L. Merryweather Handal wrote:

The stalwart Texan stepped out of the raging blizzard and into the flaming cauldron, never shirking from his duties, knowing that he must save his beautiful Virginia belle, Elizabeth, from the demonic advances of the nefarious French ruffian and his ten villainous companions.

"I shall sell this lass to the Comanches," the Frenchman spake, "but fear not, my friend, for you shall not live to see it happen."

"I think not," the Texas borderman replied, and into his hands leaped two lethal Colt Peacemakers, their twelve-inch barrels spitting flame and violent death.

Bang! Bang! Bang!

"Fear not, young Elizabeth," Colter cried out over the deafening roar of musketry as desperado

*after desperado dropped onto the snow-covered
ground and began their agonizing death throes.*

*"You soon shall be rescued, and these outlaws
will torment you and other citizens no more," our
hero continued and his words and his aim were
true, true, true.*

Bang! Bang! Bang!

That ain't exactly how it happened.

Gwen's name wasn't Elizabeth, she wasn't a belle,
and she hailed from Massachusetts, not Virginia. It
had stopped sleeting by the time I walked to the fire
to face two men, not eleven. This was 1867; Colt
Peacemakers didn't hit the market until about six years
later, and I never once saw a barrel longer than seven
and a half inches. Besides, I haven't yet learned how
to make a revolver leap into my hand.

Of course, the New York hack who wrote that novel
never once talked to me or Gwen. He just got what
he needed from West Texas saloons and made up the
rest, but the honorable Colonel L. Merryweather
Handal did get one thing right: The only reason I went
down there was because of Gwen McCarthy.

Ruisseau smiled as I limped toward him, standing
as straight as I could. He remained kneeling by the
fire, his right hand gripping the butt of the LeMat cannon in its holster. I stopped when I was parallel to
Otto, keeping the Frenchman in front of me and hook-
ing both thumbs in my sash, just inches from the Starr
revolver.

All he had to do was shoot me, or have Otto do it, but somehow I figured he'd want me to suffer first, and Alain Ruisseau loved to hear himself talk. That would give me a chance.

"Colter, *mon ami,* I am glad you have joined us at last," Ruisseau said, still smiling. "Now we can conclude our unfinished business."

I glanced at Gwen briefly, smiled, and turned my attention to Ruisseau, keeping Otto in the corner of my vision.

"Culbertson, I assume, is dead?" Ruisseau asked.

He crossed himself after my head bobbed slightly. "Tsk, tsk, but I should thank you. Eventually I would have had to kill the idiot myself. And Kate and the others?"

I shrugged.

"Your friend is a lot of trouble," Ruisseau said, turning to Gwen. "But this means more money for Otto and myself. Perhaps we shall deal with the Comanches on our own. Some brave would love to have Mademoiselle McCarthy for a squaw. Is it not so?" He was facing me again, his eyes filled with hate. He tugged on the ends of his curly mustache with his left hand. His right never moved from the LeMat.

"*Mon ami,*" he said dryly, "toss your revolver at your feet or Otto will kill the woman now."

I had positioned myself so that I could make my trick shot, but there were drawbacks. The gunshot wound in my right arm had not completely healed, several ribs were cracked, my broken fingers throbbed, and the bullet hole in my thigh burned. I was weak from the loss of blood, my head ached, and I was freezing. Worse, Otto stood on my left. In my trick shooting, I had always been on a horse and my first target had been on the right. There was nothing I could do about that now. I'd only get one chance.

I didn't want to commit suicide but I expected to die, hoping to kill Ruisseau and Otto before they finished me off. Then Jeff and the McCarthys could eventually free themselves and make it back to Franklin. My heart pounded. I tried to steady my nerves.

"The revolver, Colter," Ruisseau said. His smile vanished. "Otto!" he barked. "Shoot the woman. Right between—"

My right hand jerked the Starr free and I fired from waist level across my belly, never aiming. Spinning on my heels, I extended my arm, drew a quick bead on Alain Ruisseau and shot again—not even bothering to see if my first bullet hit its mark. The gunshots sounded like one, reverberating across the rocks, causing my ears to ring. It was over in less than two seconds.

Otto had doubled over with a bullet in his heart, the Spencer repeater, unfired, pitching from his dead arms. Ruisseau sat motionless by the fire, his expression unchanged except for the small hole that now appeared on the bridge of his nose. His mouth was open—he had always talked too much—but he no longer spoke so I completed his sentence for him.

"The eyes," I said, and he fell forward.

I breathed again. When the barrel of my Starr cooled, I shoved the gun in my sash and slowly checked on the two killers. Both were dead, and suddenly a strange emotion overcame me. I sighed, then laughed. *It had been so easy!* It wasn't that I found killing funny, even men like Ruisseau and Otto. Maybe I was just a little crazy after all I had been through and was laughing at still being alive.

Gwen McCarthy wasn't so amused. "Hey!" she shouted. "Untie us! It's freezing out here!"

I laughed again, but for a different reason, found a knife, and cut the McCarthys and Jeff loose. While Mr. McCarthy bandaged Jeff's head wound, Gwen and I embraced. She apologized for snapping at me. I said I was sorry for getting her into so much trouble.

Slowly we walked back to the Butterfield station. I found a bottle of whiskey in the corner and took a stiff drink. I needed one.

That afternoon, I buried the soldiers behind the adobe station and rolled Ruisseau and the other outlaws into a common grave a half mile away, covering their bodies with rocks. There was a sizable reward for those men, but I had no stomach for bounty hunting. I hadn't killed Ruisseau for money. If Jeff or someone else wanted to lead the authorities to the grave for identification and collect the bounty, that was fine with me.

I did, however, collect on the rewards for Waxahachie Kate, Henri, and Larry. It all totaled to about two hundred dollars, which I wired to Kate's husband in San Antonio, suggesting he use it on a lawyer or to raise his daughter. He used it on an attorney, but not the way I expected. He filed for divorce.

Kate spent two years in prison, then lit a shuck for Arizona Territory and got into more trouble, resulting in more half-dime novels. In newspapers, I read various stories where she got killed robbing a bank in Contention City, disappeared into South America, or found religion and was a missionary in the Philippines. None of those I believed. I got a letter from her about six months ago. She said she was dealing faro in Alaska and proud of her daughter's accomplishments in Dodge City. Now that rang true.

Gwen wouldn't let me keep the letter.

Henri died of consumption in prison within a year, and Larry was hanged after a speedy trial in Franklin. Jeff Crutchfield went home to his wife, who delivered him a beautiful daughter. A year later, they had another girl. He's raising horses and kids in the Davis Mountains these days, and staying a little closer to home. Every once in a while, however, he'll take off to the Guadalupes or, more often, a nearby saloon.

Stephen McCarthy left his daughter in Franklin and returned to Boston, saying he was going to reopen his photographer's studio and that he had experienced enough of the West to last him a lifetime. He says he has never taken a drop of liquor since, and I believe him. These days, he's busy with a temperance league in Boston. That's the gospel truth.

* * *

We stayed at Heuco Tanks for another day, then loaded up our prisoners and horses and moved out for Franklin. I helped Mr. McCarthy into the "What-Is-It Wagon" and turned to Gwen. We looked at each other for a long time. I took her right hand in mine and smiled.

She was a beautiful woman. My proposal in the desert had been far from romantic, so I slowly dropped to one knee and said softly, "I was serious about marrying you, Gwen McCarthy. If you'll have me."

Tears welled in her eyes. "I'd be proud to marry you," she whispered. I rose and we hugged. She brushed away tears, laughed, and looked up at Mr. McCarthy.

"Father," she asked, "does it surprise you that you'll have a son-in-law once we reach Franklin?"

The old man laughed and waved his hand in a scoffing gesture. "Daughter," he said, "I knew that when I was drunk. Any fool could see that you two mule heads are made for each other."

I kissed Gwen gently and would have held her longer, but Waxahachie Kate spoiled the mood.

"Hey, Rosebud!" she shouted. "You gonna invite me to the nuptials?"

I should have left the gag in her mouth, but the United States marshal probably wouldn't allow it, I thought as I helped Gwen into the wagon beside her father.

"It's about thirty or so miles to Franklin," I said. "Let's get going."

Suddenly Gwen slapped her forehead.

"What is it?" I asked.

"Oh, no!" she replied. "Photographs."

Thinking that I understood, I nodded. "We never got that picture of a mountain lion," I said. "But we can come back."

Gwen looked at me and smiled. "No, silly," she said. "Not that. Who's going to take our wedding portrait?"

Stephen McCarthy cleared his throat. "Me," he answered.